MW01659862

Alter Ego

A NOVEL

Monique Bledsoe

Acknowledgements

Dreams may only be figments of the imagination, but having the passion to follow them is real. It is God I thank for blessing me with the family, friends and experiences that he has, and I am grateful to all of them. To the many of you that witnessed or contributed to the creation of Alter Ego, I thank you. To those of you who supported me, my appreciation is indefinite. To my dear sister, Andrea Blair, your contributions to this project are greater than you could ever know, and as my graphic designer, I thank you. To my editor, Lesley Neff, your efforts are very much appreciated and it is a pleasure working with you.

Also, I have learned that so many factors go into writing and publishing a novel. So in addition to thanking my technical supporters; I would also like to thank my Mom, my Dad and My b-i-l. To my baby brother, I love you and I know that you can do anything you put your mind to. To Chyla, Kelli, Brandi, and Terri, thank you so much for your help. To my friend*sss,* this calls for a celebration!

With Love

Part I

Confusion vs. Prophecy

"Images have the unique ability to inspire one without explanation. What so ever those images are perceived to be, create an immediate idea. A collection of images will force our brains to contemplate order and meaning, to foster understanding. Until those images are clear, our minds are at constant battle between prophecy and confusion."

One

With a sharp kick to the abdomen, Kirsten stumbled backwards, trying to catch her balance. She braced herself on the wall just long enough to plant one foot and return the other with a fierce blow to his chest. She watched as one of the men who had launched an attack on her fell backwards.

She realized that there were three men, in total, throwing casual punches, as if they weren't really trying to hit hard and jumping around like they were aiming to tire her out. Once she had evaded them, she ran towards a staircase that appeared to be the only way out of her ordeal. The situation itself seemed to have an essence of surrealism, and as much as she would like to believe that she could handle three men, none of it seemed to be true.

As she made her way up the stairs, she could see a light coming from over the top of the landing. She squinted her eyes and continued to focus on the bright area when suddenly, she felt the waist of her pants being pulled backwards. She turned over on her back, kicking and gritting her teeth to be let go. Her final kick landed on her attacker's face, and she scurried up the stairs. Just before she reached the landing, she saw a woman standing in front of a large crowd. She was wearing a red dress and standing next to a man in a dark suit. Kirsten glanced over the audience of people in the room, as she wondered what she was looking at. In seconds, she felt herself being tossed backwards. She slid down the stairs, rolling onto one of her adversaries and then, the floor. Two of the men stood around her, looking as if they were ready to attack. Kirsten didn't stop to think about the third man; she simply assumed a fighting posture and walked slightly to her right to position both men to the front of her. As the first man charged, she felt anxiety run through her body, and as she moved to escape his blow, she seemed to be blacking out.

Kirsten shook her head to regain focus and in the process, she saw the third man standing behind her, dangling a shiny object. As she blacked in and out, she felt her eyes opening; once she realized that she was waking up, she closed her eyes tight to be sure her opponent couldn't get the best of her. After knocking the first man to the ground, the other charged forward, meeting her hands as she grabbed his neck, throwing him down towards her knee. Out of the corner of her eye, she saw the third man running towards her quickly and noticed that his shiny object was a knife. Before her other opponent even hit the ground, she felt the cold steel as it came closer and closer to her skin. She panicked as she drew the conclusion that they were really trying to harm her. She began trying to scream for help, but no matter how hard she tried, nothing came out. Her mouth moved and veins flexed from her neck, but there was no sound.

Her mind raced, as she wondered what was really going on. It raced even more when she realized that she had become helpless. She felt the cold steel, and immediately, she thought back to the lady in the red dress.

Why didn't anyone hear the commotion? Why hadn't anyone offered help? she thought, as she stood paralyzed like a deer in headlights.

The three men didn't seem as though they had set out for her; they just seemed to be there. The fight didn't seem malicious just as though it was their nature. None of the specifics mattered; at the time, they had gotten her. Her voice went from a forceful, silent yell to a loud, screeching, ear piercing shriek, being accompanied by a baby's cry.

Aubrey, Kirsten's big sister, stood over her, as the loud screeching yell came from her mouth. Kirsten opened her eyes to see her sister standing over her, holding her crying daughter's head to her chest and covering her little ears. Kirsten blinked a few times, as she attempted to make the image standing over her clear, making sure that she wasn't having another dream.

"Wow! Why did you scream like that, what's wrong with you?" said Aubrey.

Kirsten just looked at her with fear in her eyes, as she tried to focus on her sister.

"I was just saying Happy New Year; were you having a bad dream or something, dang?! You act like somebody was trying to kill you," Aubrey joked.

"Sorry," said Kirsten, as she tried to make sense of what was going on.

"It's alright; you just have to get my little sweat pea to stop crying," replied Aubrey in a baby voice.

Aubrey handed her little sister the baby and started off towards the family room. As Kirsten tried to calm her niece, she realized it wasn't working. Kirsten was still shaking from the trauma of her dream, and little Blair could tell; she insisted on crying louder and louder, until she felt safe.

Aubrey reached for her baby, as their mom, Kim asked, “Why all the screaming? I know I didn’t raise a bunch of banshees.”

“Your daughter is passing her psychosis to my child,” said Aubrey.

“Both of you are crazy!” said Kirsten’s little brother, Austin, who was sitting right next to his mom on the couch.

“Shut up, momma’s boy!” Kirsten mumbled, as she poured water from the refrigerator.

Kirsten had met her entire family at their home for the holidays. Like usual, when they where home, they enjoyed each other’s company so much that it brought back constant reminders of when they were children and couldn’t get along. Kirsten’s brother in law, Devin even played a long. He was almost as good at relating to them as the three that grew up together, only he had an advantage. He and his wife, Aubrey, were usually a team.

“Kirsten, why are you screaming?” asked her mom, determined to get an answer as to what was going on.

“I don’t know. She just scared me,” Kirsten said, as she tried to move past the recent event.

Aubrey continued to joke with Austin, as she sat next to her husband on the loveseat. Devin was able to get his little girl to stop crying in seconds. She just curled right up on her daddy’s chest, like most infants would, and closed her little, almond eyes.

The siblings laughed and teased each other from room to room, until their mom chimed in, saying "I came in the kitchen not to have to listen to my adult children acting like kids. You wake your dad up, and we'll see who has the last laugh."

Austin Sr. had worked a night shift, and he had been asleep since the first of his children had walked in the door. Kirsten secretly hoped they had awakened him so that he could join in. She just didn't want to get blamed for it, but she would have loved to have someone take her side.

Nevertheless, he was awake. Even if he were still sleepy, he couldn't willingly go back to bed, knowing his children, whom he rarely got to see, were home.

Austin Sr. came down the stairs into the family room where everyone had convened and said, "The loudest one is cooking dinner." Everyone laughed and pointed at Kirsten to do the task. Kim, her mom said, "Well, Aubrey was up there torturing the girl in her sleep. I say they should share the job, for old time sake."

Kirsten replied, "Fine, I'll take dinner, if she does breakfast."

"Okay," Aubrey agreed, just before Kirsten said, "I wanted pizza anyway."

"No, that's not fair. You have to cook. Devin and I aren't eating fast food this year. That's our New Years Resolution," said Aubrey.

"Well, you two will just have to cook for yourselves, cause if she's getting pizza, I'm on her side," said Austin.

"Pizza has all the food groups anyway, and it's baked its not fast food," said Kirsten.

New Years Eve is usually the day people decide to do all the things they've been trying to do all year but never quite get around to, especially in Kirsten's family. She had attempted her own New Years Resolutions a few times; this last year, it was to eat healthy. The year before that, it was to attend church; before that, it was to stop drinking. She had her own failed attempts at resolutions, and this year was to be the last of them. This year, she felt as if it would be the resolution to end all yearly resolutions. It would be so profound that she could live her life completely satisfied and completely empowered to do or change anything she wanted, on any given day.

Kirsten had no plans as to what the New Year would bring, but nothing could keep her from thinking the best. She was finally her own person with her own life, and as long as she worked hard at what she wanted, it could only get better.

The family sat around the dinner table that had been set for a typical family event and said grace over a not so typical meal. They passed the boxes of pizza around, as Mom said, "This is the type of meal I like, one that I don't have to slave over making or spend hours cleaning up after."

Everyone laughed, until Dad said, "Well, let's hear these resolutions you all have been bugging me about."

"You first, Dad," said Kirsten.

"I made mine already," said her Dad.

"Well, let's hear them," said Aubrey.

"You are looking at it; I made a resolution to see my children grow old. That's as much as I could ask for," he said.

"That's cheating, Dad," said Aubrey.

"Well, this year, I'm gonna spend more time with your brother, before he gets out there in this world."

"What world? He's gonna come stay with one of us," said Aubrey.

Kirsten sat there silently, as she contemplated her own resolution. She had seriously been thinking about what she could do to make life better for herself, but she was drawing a blank.

"Kirsten, your turn," said her mother.

"How am I next? You're cheating now! You were next," said Kirsten.

"No, sweetie, we are going around the table," replied her mom.

Kirsten took a deep breath and decided just to say anything. She didn't like the idea of not participating, but she couldn't think of a worthwhile resolution. She flashed an innocent smile, saying "I will see my family more often."

Everyone smiled and went on to the next. The younger Austin said, "I am going to save more money and stop shopping."

His dad looked at him and smiled, saying "Now you learn the value of a dollar; why couldn't you have learned years ago? Save me some money!"

They all laughed and continued to go around the table. Once the resolutions were done, they continued their usual conversation about their family's history and comedic outtakes. For the time being, Kirsten had forgotten about making a legitimate resolution. Of course, she would try to see her family more, but she was more inclined to finding out the secret to a perfect life.

Two

It was already two days into the New Year. Kirsten had come back to her apartment in the city; she still hadn't set her mind on a resolution. She hadn't even thought about it on her trip home. Her life had become so mundane that her own complacency bothered her. The only thing exciting that had happened in her life, recently, was her bad dream. She sat and wondered if her dream had anything to do with her resolution, but she couldn't quite put her finger on it. The fact that she hadn't been allowed to finish it made her think even more about what would have happened.

Remembering back to her dream, Kirsten wondered, why was she fighting? She had never been a confrontational person before, maybe a little over protective, but that's it. Why had they even started fighting? Who were these men? Kirsten worried herself, looking for the answer to her questions for hours, until she decided to take her mind off of the dream. She didn't feel at all comfortable thinking about why someone would be after her, especially not living by herself.

She did everything she could to stay preoccupied which included her taking out clothes to iron for work while she watched television. She stood there looking for something casual but couldn't find anything. She had been groomed in college to dress the part, especially if she wanted to be a professional, and so she did. The bad part about it was that the job she found after college only required casual clothes, so as long as she didn't have on jeans, she could pretty much wear whatever she wanted.

Thinking of her job's dress code made her think of what she was doing there in the first place. She had taken the job simply for the sake of working. She hadn't forgotten what she wanted to do in her life; she just needed to figure out how to do it. Now, she knew that her current job wasn't the best way to get there. As the days went by, she walked further and further down a dead end.

Kirsten went through the same thing every time she picked her clothes out for work. She wanted to fit in but looking professional meant more to her. Most of Kirsten's life, she'd dreamed of being a successful businesswoman. In her eyes, that meant to be a venture capitalist. She wanted a long list of businesses that would help her bring life to the small, deprived town she grew up in. Only now, she was stuck in a meaningless nine to five and hated it. She thought it would pay the bills while she finished her business plans and researched her first opportunity, but she was miserable doing it. By the third month of her being there, it dawned on her that she had no insurance and was being paid the same as someone who didn't have a degree. Not only that, she sat across from a woman who had held the same job for twenty –two years and had seen three different bosses, all of whom she had been perfectly comfortable working with. One thing was for sure; Kirsten had a completely different take on where she wanted to end up. Angela was in her forties and had worked there twenty-two years. Her uncle started the company and hired her to help him run it. She had gone to college for a semester and decided that she didn't like it. Like Kirsten, Angela's only choice was to find a job immediately, and who better to work for than family? Kirsten thought that maybe all of the stress from running someone else's business all those years had aged her, but she didn't seem to mind.

As a mom of two teenagers, Angela was very kind and somewhat soft spoken. She was usually swamped with work, so the others never really seemed to bother her much. The one thing that really got on her nerves was Anthony; he was very nice but he never seemed to do any work. Kirsten had the feeling that he just didn't want to be there, and sure enough, he began to talk about how badly he wanted to leave. The fact that he and his boss didn't get along well probably had a lot to do with it.

Kirsten's other co-worker was pretty nice, too. She worked with a 35 year old widow named Allison who had three children and a high school diploma. Her husband was much older than her, but he passed away at 57 of a heart attack and unfortunately, didn't have any insurance for his wife, which meant she had to go back to work, but his kids had major trust funds in which she was the guardian over. Most of the time, Allison was nice to talk to, but she would always end up talking about secrets to saving money. At first, Kirsten thought she talked about money a lot, because she always had to worry about it. The longer she got to know her, that turned out not to be true at all. She shopped at discount stores and off brand shops for the everyday stuff that other people took for granted, simply because she couldn't bear to eliminate the otherwise lavish lifestyle that she learned to live with her husband. She would talk about the country club her family belonged to and the exciting trips they would take across the world. She really was an interesting person, and Kirsten began to appreciate their conversations, or at least the ones where they would talk about more cultural topics, which basically, meant anything but money.

Marc, her boss, was a nice guy, but he had his own issues. Like most bosses, he thought he was a good one, and he was for those that wanted to be there. Sometimes, he made it sound as though he was struggling financially and boasted about how the pay was good compared to others. Kirsten knew people stayed, because they were comfortable. Something was better than nothing, and the flexibility he offered was a good incentive.

Her office was almost like a small family, in the sense that they were loyal to one another, even the ones that didn't get along so well. They wouldn't take the day off and leave the others to do lots of work, unless of course, there was an emergency. Besides, they would even talk a little bit about their personal lives; for everyone else, it was about their families and what they had done back in their day, and for Kirsten, it was whether or not she dated anyone new.

They even considered themselves a small little working family during birthdays. On Kirsten's birthday, her boss ordered pizza, like he had for all the others, and their most senior employee made a cake to bring for her. Though she had only been there a short time compared to the others, he treated her like he treated everyone else in his office, like his extended family. That meant he had an idea for everything she should do in life. His favorite words where, "You see, what I would do is," and whatever followed usually ended in something not so politically correct.

Kirsten had taken more than her fair share of HR classes in college, enough so that she wouldn't offend anyone. She wasn't certain her boss knew anything about workplace conduct, because he'd said a few things that she wasn't quite sure as to whether or not she was offended. Until that one day in January! She woke up, thinking her day would be great, only to get halfway through it and realize that it was a downhill ride.

This time, she woke up on time, in contrast to the last couple of months, when she rolled out of bed with just enough time to rush through her morning routine. She made her way to the office and even had time to stop for breakfast at the drive-thru. Kirsten walked into the office and gave everyone her usual cheerful greeting, while she sat at her computer, waiting for it to boot. She started to do her two favorite things before her workload picked up, which were to research opportunities for her business ideas and look for another job. She usually felt bad about looking stuff up during the workday, but she got over it when she realized that she didn't have much to do and that it was better than getting caught sleeping. Kirsten wanted to do work that she enjoyed, and servicing insurance wasn't her idea of a dream job.

She sat there a whole two hours before her boss came in at his usual time. At that moment, she thought to herself, she wanted that same control over her career. She kept thinking of what Gordon Parks said, "The guy who takes a chance, who walks the line between the known and the unknown, who is unafraid of failure, will succeed." Sure, her boss had some responsibilities, but he had the luxury of making decisions and not running them by anyone else. He controlled his income, his hours and everything that went along with it.

Kirsten said hello to him, as she closed the internet window. She had been searching for jobs online and kept her mind weighing on where her success would be. She sat the rest of the morning, thinking of the opportunities that were out there, and the afternoon daydreaming of her friends, her boyfriends and her job or the job she was looking for. At about 3:00 p.m., the office started to get really busy, so dreaming of her ideal night out, after her ideal day of work, had to wait.

She entered request after request for her boss's customers, and by the hour's end, things were slow again. By that time, she'd talked to her fair share of people who demanded to speak to the same boss who told her not to let anyone's talk bother him.

The last man who walked in, demanding to speak to his agent, sat in front of her and said, "I'll sit here until he comes out to talk to me."

Kirsten looked at him with exhaustion on her face. She didn't care if he talked to him or not; it wasn't her fault that when she called her boss on his line, he said, "See if you can help him first. He probably doesn't need to talk to me." It was obvious that he had no plans on helping the angry guy, and the more he sat there, the angrier he got.

Kirsten called her bosses extension, saying "Marc, I really do think you should speak with this customer."

Marc huffed and said, “Fine, I’ll be just a second.”

Her boss came out, and they greeted each other like old college buddies, like he hadn’t just insisted on not talking with the man, and then, chatted a little before her boss asked what he needed. He stood right over Kirsten, the whole time telling her what to do, instead of going into his office to do the job quicker himself.

Once they were done helping the guy, he stood up to join Kirsten’s boss, who was standing behind her, and they chatted some more; this time, he was asking how business was going. Her boss took his usual stand in saying, “You know it could be going better, it’s been kind of slow.” Just as Kirsten was thinking that he was such a liar and that they had been busier than ever, he spoke again, saying “Maybe if I put Kirsten outside in a bathing suit, business will get a little better.” Kirsten bit her tongue. Once she felt the shock from his words, she was disgusted and at the same time, happy that the workday was over.

He stood behind her, chuckling with his customer about the stupid remark he’d made. Kirsten stood up from her desk and walked straight to the door. She didn’t turn to look at him, she didn’t wave, and she didn’t say good-bye; she just left. When Kirsten got in the car, she started out thinking how offended, how embarrassed she was. When he said those words, it took her back to a place in her mind that she had been that past summer, when she worked with Steve, the meat man.

Kirsten had been looking for other sales jobs for a good month, before she found the job with Marc, when she’d finally gotten a call back. She’d done an interview over the phone, which seemed legitimate, and then, they scheduled a face-to-face interview. At her interview, she wore a suit, and everyone else was dressed in the usual business casual. Kirsten did her research, and the company was legitimate, only their distribution was not quite how it appeared to be from her research. Kirsten thought she had accepted a position as a representative, to go to stores and restaurants that the company had contracts with and convince them to purchase more of their products. Little did she know, she would show up to the distribution site, only to find that she had accepted a door-to-door sales job.

On her first day, she had dressed down to meet their business casual standards, but when she arrived, the other so-called-reps were wearing jeans and sweat suits. They paired her with a 40 something man named Steve, who had been doing the job for nearly 10 years. The first thing he said was "I bet you didn't know you'd be doing door to door sales."

Kirsten answered with a flustered, "No. No I didn't." Perhaps he could tell by the look on her face that she was as surprised as they came.

"They do that to people all the time; they get these young college kids and give them the impression that they'll have a real white collar job, and then, they send them down here for us to tell them the damn truth. Some of the guys do it for a little while, but a pretty little girl like you… I'll tell you what, I gotta load the truck. You take some time to think about it, and if you ain't at the truck in ten minutes, I'll leave without you," said Steve.

Kirsten took a deep breath and remembered that she hadn't found another job yet. She bit her lip and decided that she had run out of time; she could try it at least, long enough to pay her bills and keep looking for something else. She headed through the door, not too long after Steve, on her way to the truck.

"So, you decided to come along anyway, huh! That a girl," he said.

"I guess it won't hurt to try it; I'm already here, right," Kirsten retorted, looking around at all the other trucks. Most of the employees were younger men and middle aged, rough looking women, but they all drove newer work trucks than he did.

Soon after they pulled out of the lot in a dingy oversized pickup truck, they stopped at a hole in the wall diner. Steve leaned over towards Kirsten and said, "Hey doll, how about some breakfast?"

Kirsten leaned away and replied, "I'm not hungry, but I'll wait for you." He took the keys out of the truck after rolling up the windows, which Kirsten took to mean that she couldn't sit and wait for him. She got out and followed him into the restaurant, hoping that he would just eat and leave; instead, he ate and talked the whole time.

Kirsten didn't like the tone he had progressed toward in the last five minutes, and aside from being highly annoyed that her job hunt was such a bust, she really wasn't in much of a talking mood. However, that didn't stop Steve from running his mouth. After ordering his food, he sat across from her at the table and said, "So, you seeing anybody?"

Kirsten looked at him oddly and said, "I have a few friends."

Steve laughed and replied, "You remind me of my sister, only she's not half as pretty as you, and she's a little skinny."

"Excuse me!" Kirsten replied.

"Well, she used to do that friend thing; she'd have all the guys paying her bills and taking her shopping. I knew you had to be single, because no guy in his right mind would have you out here working. What you need is somebody who can take care of you. If I were your 'so-called-friend', you'd be out shopping."

Kirsten took an arrogant frame of mind and thought to herself that there was no way in hell he would be one of her 'friends', and a meat man definitely couldn't be her type.

"Well, Steve, I can take care of myself. Besides, I didn't expect this job to be what it is, and under any other circumstance, I wouldn't be here."

Steve blew right passed her statement and continued on his own agenda. "Have you every dated anyone older than you? I mean like 46?" asked Steve.

"No," Kirsten snapped back before quickly changing the subject. "So, what did you do before this?" asked Kirsten.

"I worked in sales for a few different companies, mostly auto parts. When my wife took my kids and everything I had in my divorce, I needed to make some extra money. So, when selling meat on the weekends got better than selling timing belts during the week, I quit."

Kirsten knew she needed to control the conversation just long enough to keep him from asking her more ridiculous questions. "How old are your kids?" asked Kirsten.

"My boy is 26, and my daughter is 22."

She thought it was strange that a man who had two kids could bring himself to hit on someone a little older than his own daughter. Unfortunately, she spent too much time thinking, because Steve asked her, "So, what are you looking for in man; I know you don't want to be single forever."

"I'm not looking for anything; I like my life the way it is," lied Kirsten with a straight face.

After the tone Kirsten took with Steve, they didn't really talk the rest of the day. Steve did his job as usual, and Kirsten, tolerantly, listened to his old rock hits while praying the day went by a little faster.

By 2:00, she had almost forgotten how much of a pig he had been, until they stopped at the gas station. Steve got out and pumped gas; when he finished, he walked around to tap on her window, "I'm going in for some hotdogs. You want anything; you haven't eaten all day?"

"No thanks," she said. Kirsten didn't have an appetite; she was kind of upset that she had wasted the whole day doing a job she never planned to come back to. Steve walked away from the window; then, he turned back around before Kirsten had the opportunity to roll the window back up.

"Are you sure you don't wanna blow off the rest of the day and get a hotel room?"

Kirsten's mouth dropped; she had never been asked such a thing, even the raunchy boys back in grade school who'd tried to get with her had better taste than that. Kirsten gritted her teeth and said, "Hell, no! Take me back, NOW!"

Steve turned around and walked into the gas station. He acted as though he hadn't just sexually harassed someone. Kirsten had never been accosted by anyone in that manner, and to her, it felt rather uncomfortable. She suddenly felt dizzy and sick to her stomach. She couldn't believe he had asked her such a thing and thought maybe she was nauseous, because he was so disgusting. She wondered if she had encouraged it in some way or if she could have handled it a better way.

All Kirsten could do to fight the tears was to mentally block what had just happened. She felt terrible inside. She wanted to get out and walk, but she had no idea what community she was in. She had never seen this part of town and couldn't remember the route he had taken.

He walked out of the gas station casually and hopped in the truck to say, "Ready to go," as if nothing had happened. Kirsten cut her eyes at him and looked out of the window. As soon as he started the truck, Kirsten realized she was in one of those situations her mom told her never to put herself in. She was in a car with a man that she didn't know anything about, who had basically been harassing her since the day started. Anything could happen to her. She rode the whole way back with her cell phone in her hand in case she had to jump out and call someone quickly.

The entire ride back to the office was silent. Kirsten got out of the truck, slammed the door and walked quickly towards her car. Steve, once again, took his casual stroll to the door, as he turned to her and said, "You coming back tomorrow."

Kirsten didn't believe he had just asked her that. She slid in her car and turned on the engine, just as soon as she could, her car ripped out of the parking lot as though she were in a racecar at the starting line.

Halfway home, Kirsten realized that she was really upset, and her tears were probably a good indication of that. By the time Kirsten reached her apartment, she wiped her face so that no one could see that she had been crying. She walked in and went straight for her room; all she could think of was to lie down. She dropped all of her things at the door. She didn't even take her shoes off; she just flew onto her bed and cried. About five minutes after she got home, her phone rang. Her sister wanted to find out about her first day on the job. She answered the phone only because if she didn't, it would be ringing all day.

Kirsten told her sister she had a bad day and that she just wanted to lie down. Of course, Aubrey didn't let it go that easily; she insisted Kirsten tell her what happened, and then, she would let her go to sleep. Kirsten rehashed the whole day in a quick 60 second synopsis, only to have her mom call 10 minutes later. She knew it was nice to have people who cared about her, but it wasn't so nice when all she wanted to do was sleep and forget about that day's events. Her mom tried to act as if she hadn't just gotten off the phone with her sister, but Kirsten could tell in her voice that she was concerned. So, she played the game. After her mom said "Hello, Daughter," she cheerfully replied "Hello, Mother".

Her mother said, "What you doing?"

"I am lying down; what are you doing?" Kirsten replied.

The cheery conversation continued for a little while, until her mom figured out how to bring her new job up. After Kirsten told her everything, her mom admitted that she had already heard the news from her other daughter.

"Are you going to tell your dad?" her mother asked.

"Uhm, I really don't want to talk about it. I just want to go to sleep," said Kirsten.

"Well, he's here if you want to talk to him," her mom said.

Kirsten just knew if he was there, he already knew. She was annoyed that each and every person had to have his or her own individual account as to what happened. The story was the same when she told her sister, her mother and more than likely, when her sister finished telling all of her own close friends and relatives; it was all the same story that every one seemed to want her to relive, just so they could hear it from the horse's mouth.

By the time she turned the corner, she was fed up with thinking of being offended. She dropped one single crocodile tear and remembered that she had shed more tears in corporate America than she'd ever shed as a child. With that, she spent the rest of the ride home, trying to put together the words "I quit!" She hadn't found a job but needed to, and hopefully, she would soon.

Kirsten got home and immediately started to look for work; she had narrowed down a few opportunities that would train her, but then, let her be her own boss. By midnight, she had decided on being a Financial Advisor. This wasn't the first time she had looked at being a Financial Advisor. She could remember telling her dad that she wanted to, and he said, "I know how to count my own money, I'm not gone pay somebody to do it. Why don't you be an architect or a lawyer?" Her dad had his point, in which he probably understood, but Kirsten just accepted it and started looking for another career. For a seven year old, that was easy, because she really wanted to be a gymnast. She didn't know anyone who had done it before her and practically couldn't wait to call the company the next day and see how to apply.

Three

The next day came, and Kirsten woke up in a shiny disposition. She didn't march right in her boss's office to say I quit quite like she wanted to; she decided to wait until she'd at least found out what it would take for the new job. She worked silently, when she had to, but sat drawing doodles of her dreams, until her phone rang.

Kirsten was really the only person who answered the phone, and usually, it wasn't for her. This time, it was. On the other end was some guy who she'd met marketing for her company. Their boss had given them each a list of apartments and car lots in which they were to go and hand out treats and info on his business; that was the only part of her job that was close to being the sales rep that she thought she was hired to be.

A few weeks back, she'd remembered going to one apartment community and being greeted by a young guy. She was glad he was there as opposed to the other ladies that usually answered the door, because they were extremely obnoxious and rude. Josh was sort of a breath of fresh air. Apparently, he had gotten more out of their meeting than she did, because he was calling to invite her to see him play basketball.

Kirsten thought to herself momentarily about how stupid the guy sounded on the other end, and as soon as it showed on her face, the words poured out of her mouth, "No, thanks, I have plans for this evening." The clueless, young man accepted her answer, and she moved on with her life. Kirsten thought of all of the athletes she had dated in her life who couldn't move past their own obsession with sports in order to connect with a real person, who wasn't obsessed with keeping score. Kirsten was glad she had said no and wouldn't change her mind for anything. Besides, she didn't even know this guy, and he definitely knew nothing about dating; she was convinced she'd have a bad time anyway.

She continued the rest of the day, doodling on her pad of paper, as there was little work for her to do. Luckily for her, the phone rang again; only this time, it was the recruiter from the company she had applied to. He seemed so excited to talk with her, almost as excited as she was. They scheduled a meeting between the two of them for the beginning of next week, and both went about their days.

Kirsten was so excited to go to work that she had gotten up extremely early to make sure she left nothing behind. She needed to bring her resume and her jacket for her suit. She couldn't wear a suit to work, or her boss would be all in her business, trying to see where she was going. She decided to put it in her car and just put it on when she got to her meeting.

Kirsten made it to work just in time. Her boss seemed to be having an early day and whenever she was late he was early, so being there just at 8:29 was good enough for her. She walked in and put her things at her desk and continued to walk past her boss's office saying "Morning". Her mom had taught her that it never hurt to speak to anyone. So even though she didn't feel like wishing him a good morning or saying a cheery 'Hi or Hello', she still knew better than to ignore him completely.

Noon had come around, and she was all too ready to get off to her meeting and see about the job she had been so excited about. She had tried most of her life to follow her heart or her instinct, whatever it was that had always helped her to make good decisions. This job seemed like the one that would make her successful. It seemed to be her way to reach the "American Dream".

That was a concept she got from her dad. He probably never said those words, but in her way of figuring out why he worked so hard, she stumbled upon the concept. Her daddy was a cop; he actually had a bunch of different jobs. He worked with real estate, and he owned a delivery company run by her mom. Her dad told her stories of the things he wanted to do in life and the opportunities he wanted to invest in. Kirsten looked up to her dad, as if he knew everything, and though he didn't, he did know quite a bit. His experiences led him to the comfort zone that he lived in. Some of his stories were a little depressing, especially when he'd talk about the things he should have done and the things life had prevented him from doing, but her mom balanced them out every time. She told Kirsten that she could do whatever she put her mind to.

Kirsten reached her destination on the north side of the city. It was conveniently placed in the middle of all of the major suburbs, where wealthy people seemed to flock home after a day at their big offices. She went up to the 15th floor, where she had been instructed to meet her potential employers. She sat in the lobby and waited almost ten minutes for the man who had promised to meet with her and watched several others walk by as she sat. Jim, the man she had been talking with over the phone, came out to greet her. “Hi, I’m Jim,” he said, as he extended his hand. “Hello, I’m Kirsten,” she said. She shook his hand, as she noticed how awkward he stood.

She had been talking to Jim an entire five minutes and had completely figured him out. He seemed to be very book smart, but he couldn’t speak well, as his vocabulary was fine, but he never connected with Kirsten. She knew, then, that he was in management for one reason and one reason only; he couldn’t sell. After getting all of the information he needed from Kirsten, he called in another guy named Brad. Brad was a medium height, older gentleman with a balding head. He almost reminded Kirsten of that old puppet from the Muppet Babies, but when he spoke, he was very impressive. His diction was impeccable, and his posture was strong. He began to connect with Kirsten, unlike the first guy Jim, but he seemed to keep looking at her shoulder. He took his hand, as if he was gesturing “okay” and slowly picked a piece of glitter off of her shoulder, saying “You seemed to have sat too close to the plant in the lobby.” Kirsten couldn’t believe that he was so meticulous, but she hoped that his OCD issues would help her to learn everything she needed to know about his business. She was told that she would meet the others if the time came for her to work there, and with that, she was content. She left the office with what seemed to be homework and a bright idea of what her career could be.

Everything the two gentlemen told her they were looking for Kirsten seemed to have an abundance of. She was more than capable of meeting people and creating relationships with them. She learned quickly and was very good at giving presentations, not to mention her time management skills could not have been better. If they would provide people for her to talk to and the training she needed, she would have no problem being a great advisor someday.

Kirsten made it back to her office with about two hours left of the workday and was reminded by her office manager that she would be going to lunch with her boss for her employment review the next day. She was excited about it, because she knew she had done a wonderful job, up until a few days ago, when she realized that she didn't belong there. Her dreams took her far beyond the walls that were now around her. She sat the last two hours, researching the career she would go into and the company's reputation that would be branded on her upon employment.

Kirsten had been at work only a few minutes when a familiar young man walked into the office. She was hoping that this wasn't one of those days when the phone would ring constantly, but she'd rather that than to have a bunch of walk-ins. She hated days like that, especially when she didn't feel like being there in the first place. The young man said, "Hey, do you remember me?"

"Uh, no, but can I help you with anything?" she replied

It was Josh; he was coming in again to ask her to watch him at his game the next day.

Kirsten was slightly annoyed that he insisted on having her watch him play basketball and even more annoyed that he just popped up at her job. She thought to herself that it couldn't be the newest trend in dating. She wondered what happened to dinner and lunches or plays, something they could both enjoy, not her watching him dribble an orange ball up and down a court full of overgrown kids. What happened to a little notice; why the day before?

"I'm not exactly a fan of adult sports recreation, but thanks anyway," Kirsten said.

The room was silent for a moment, until he finally said, "Okay, I can understand that, maybe one day."

"Well, thanks for thinking of me. Take Care," Kirsten replied.

Kirsten wondered to herself why he kept asking her the same thing. Kirsten had little space in her mind to start dating again, especially if she had to think about it. She had always liked guys who were capable of sweeping her off her feet. So, she wasn't too excited about having someone interrupt her thoughts of her new job with self centered requests.

"Okay, well, I also need to get some insurance. I got your information off the stuff you dropped off at the office and thought I would stop by. You know, kill two birds with one stone," said Josh.

"Okay, have a seat, and let's see what we can do," said Kirsten.

Kirsten had a very good feeling that he didn't want any insurance and an even better feeling that she couldn't wait to get out of customer service. She wasn't too comfortable knowing that people knew where to find her. She asked him the necessary questions before turning to her computer, trying to see whether or not he even qualified, and from what he said, he did. Of course, when she put his information in the program, it didn't work out for him. She was kind of use to people conveniently leaving out the facts, but it didn't bother her too much because that meant she was free.

The next day came along, and Kirsten was slightly excited to get to work. She knew her boss wouldn't arrive until around 10:00 a.m., and she would be out for at least an hour and a half at lunch. Any time she spent working would be well worth her new found energy. She would do whatever it took to get the new job and had no bad feelings about leaving her old one. She spent the day, yet again, writing down ideas for her new occupation. She put together budgets from what she was told the average rep usually made, and she even itemized her wardrobe so that waking up in the morning to choose clothes to wear would be no big deal.

Once her boss had come in, he seemed to be in a bit of a hurry. He walked in saying, "Hello everyone." After everyone said hello to him, he said, "Kirsten, how about Italian at noon?"

Kirsten replied, "Sounds like a plan." They both went on about their business, he in his office, doing whatever it was he made money to do and Kirsten at her cubicle, pretending to do whatever it was that he paid her to do, because more than likely, she had already done it.

At noon, Kirsten sat at her desk in no hurry, listening to her boss shuffle papers around. She didn't know if he did that pretending to be busy or if he was the world's biggest procrastinator. He walked out and said, "Okay, let's get out of here; we are eating Italian. Does anyone want anything brought back?" It was nice of him to ask, but the employees didn't eat a lot of take out; they usually brought lunch or ate some sort of fast food on occasion. After everyone casually said no thanks, he and his newest employee headed off towards Bravino's. It was a restaurant that Kirsten had never been to, but he seemed to love. Seeing that the place was only five minutes from the office, the two of them had only made it through small talk about the best restaurants in the city. By the time the food had come, they had already talked about the goals he would set for the office, the things she had learned so far, and even managed to bet on how much longer one of the other employees would be there.

Once the waiter brought out their food, her boss asked, "So, what is it that you don't like?" Kirsten thought to herself for a moment before saying, "Well, I have to say that I have grown out of my position; I know that there would still be more to learn but I don't want to learn it. I have no interest in the work we do." Kirsten's boss sat there in silence, as Kirsten began to add, "Perhaps, before you replace me, you should consider taking some HR classes; I think that quite a few times you've said some offensive things, which you may not have known to be offensive."

Her boss paused, mid bite and asked, "Like what? I think I am a pretty easy going person."

Kirsten replied, "And, you are, but everyone doesn't always have the same religious or belief systems. You can't suggest putting your female employees out front in bathing suits to boost business." Her boss looked at her and apologized for offending her and said that he would be more mindful of the things he joked about.

At the end of the dinner, it was quite obvious to Kirsten's boss that she would be leaving soon without having either of them say it. They finished their lunch and went back to the office, Kirsten had been so brutally honest. Even if her boss hadn't decided to leave early, she would probably have to fake sick and leave herself; luckily for her, he had to pick his children up from school, so he needed to leave. Not that she felt bad about what she said, she just felt out of place saying it.

Not even the whole week had gone by, and Kirsten had finished her assignment from the initial interview with the Financial Company. She called Jim to let him know that she was done. With shock in his voice, he said, "Well, let's get you back in here next week and do your second interview. How does 8:00 a.m. on Tuesday sound?"

Kirsten accepted her appointment, saying "Sounds good; I will see you at 8 a.m. on Tuesday."

Kirsten went home from work that Friday excited, so excited that sitting still watching TV wasn't going to work for her. She needed to get out, to have some fun, and to burn off some energy. Kirsten walked into her empty apartment, throwing her coat on the back of the couch. She washed her hands and immediately picked up the phone to call her friend, Robin to see what was going on that weekend. Once she reached her, she learned that because it was so cold out, no one really had plans on going anywhere. Not just because the roads were covered in ice but even if you were standing outside waiting for a cab, you would freeze your life away.

Kirsten began to tell Robin about her day and the new job she wanted. Robin had just gotten off the phone with their friends, Evelyn and Elle. They all agreed that all of them needed to go out for a drink but for different reasons, and knowing that all of them had plans on drinking, none of them wanted to be the designated driver.

Kirsten loved her friends and knew that each of them would go to the end of the earth and back for one another and anyone else for that matter. They met volunteering at a habitat for humanity project and had so much fun working together that they went out for drinks. Each time they went out, they seemed to come up with something else they should do together, and their friendship had grown ever sense.

Robin and Kirsten had actually gone to college together, so they knew each other quite well. They had a few mutual friends and would end up hanging out at times.

As a matter of fact, they had become better friends than they had ever been in college and Evelyn and Elle were the perfect constituents.

Robin had the greatest idea; she said, “Let’s go get some snacks and some drinks and have a little sleepover over at my place; that way we can all drink and take a cab downtown. Then, neither of us has to drive home.” Kirsten agreed and rushed Robin off the phone so that she could get ready. She grabbed her coat to go out for her party stuff. She would need to get some sort of dessert before she headed to the party, and double chocolate cake sounded really good. Only, she had the bright idea to inject rum in the cake and put it back in the oven so that it wouldn’t be soggy. Kirsten came home to finish her cake and get her clothes together.

It had been quite some time since Kirsten had been to a sleepover, and as juvenile as it sounded, she knew it would be far from childish. From the plans the ladies had made, it sounded like they would get together for cocktails, watch a bunch of movies and then, play some drinking games. Kirsten knew the movies wouldn’t go over too well, because whenever she got together with Elle, Robin and Evelyn, they would end up talking more than the people in the movie. Kirsten didn’t care. She just looked forward to having fun with her friends.

Once at Robin’s, she realized she was the last to get there, which may have had something to do with her friends all living on the same side of town or at least within twenty minutes of one another. Kirsten had to drive almost half an hour to get there. They were all talking about what happened since their last get together. Evelyn was expecting a surprise engagement that her fiancés mom couldn't wait to tell her about. Before they talked about Evelyn, they were talking about Elle's most recent dating experience. Her date just so happened to be with a minister who acted, spoke and carried himself like a pimp. Kirsten insisted on hearing about her date with him; she couldn't imagine how he would have told her he was a minister and a male whore in the same sitting.

Robin poured Kirsten a drink of whatever it was that Evelyn had made. She was known for her toxic concoctions, and it more than likely had at least three types of liquor in it. While Evelyn talked, Elle stood over the counter, taking out the food for them to snack on. They had more food and drinks than they could possibly ingest, especially since they all had so many interesting stories to tell.

Elle completed her story about Minster Rodney, whom had only taken her out to dinner to get his favors in return. He had no qualms about asking for what he wanted once he had his almighty hat on, which obviously didn't make him any better than anyone else, because he couldn't seem to control his urges. Robin was glad that she met him for dinner as opposed to him picking her up. After he put all of his cards on the table, Elle left him sitting there with his ego and the bill.

The group of friends sat in the kitchen for over an hour, exchanging experiences and joking about the irony in their lives.

"Okay, ladies, we might want to go downtown before we finish the party here," said Robin.

"Okay, Elle has to call the cab this time," said Evelyn.

"That's fine. I'm calling your boy with the ponytail," said Elle.

"Oh, wow. That's dirty, Elle. He is going to spend the whole time trying to see who will be his boo," said Kirsten.

"No, Kirsten, I think he has narrowed it down to you and Evelyn," said Elle.

"You're not right. At all!" said Robin." Forget it; I'll call a neutral cabby, one too old and uninterested in talking to any of us.

"Like who? Nobody catches cabs here; we only have like three cab companies in the whole city," said Kirsten.

"Fine," said Robin.

Kirsten made the call to get her friends downtown to the Wine Bar. They showed up just in time to get one of their favorite tables which were situated right next to a table of men.

"Guys, we have never been here this late; it's much emptier during the evening," said Elle.

"Well, the guys are cuter at night," joked Evelyn.

They all laughed, as they sat and noticed that everyone seemed to know each, almost like they had their own little culture.

"Anybody else notice that everyone is talking to everyone else, except for us?" asked Robin.

"Yeah, it looks that way," said Kirsten.

"We should just start talking to people. I bet they don't even know each other, just looks that way. You first, Kirsten," said Robin.

"Not a problem," said Kirsten, as she turned to talk to the guy behind her.

Kirsten held a conversation with him for about ten minutes, before she remembered that she had come with her friends. She turned and introduced her friends, and then, he did the same.

After a few rounds of drinks, the girls were ready to go. Their hangout had gotten way too crowded for their taste, and their seats where right in the middle of the mix. Robin led the way, saying "Okay, let's move this party down the street."

"Wait, let me say bye to everybody," Kirsten said giggling.

"You just want to say goodbye to that guy," said Elle.

"Maybe," said Kirsten.

She turned around and tapped her new friend on the shoulder, saying "It was nice meeting you. Maybe I'll see you here again."

"Yeah… same to you! Here, take my card; call me if you ever need anything," said Camron.

The girls headed to the restaurant next door and ate sandwiches and other quick meals; it was the only real food available after their four hour event next door. They finished their food and called the cab company to take them home; now, it was time to engage in a more obnoxious conversation about the time they had.

"Kirs, I can't believe you sat their talking to that dude the whole time you were there, like you forgot about us," said Elle.

"What? He was cute. He sounded pretty smart, too," said Kirsten.

"It's not like you gonna call him," said Evelyn.

"I might…Evelyn you didn't even see him; you where caught up with your old guy with the bald head. We always have this conversation when I talk to someone; when I don't, you want to talk about me being a party pooper. You're being hater," said Kirsten.

The girls fell asleep after trying really hard not to. They usually fell asleep mid conversation, one at a time, and the last two fell asleep after they finished teasing the others who went to sleep prematurely.

The next morning, Kirsten went straight to the nearest breakfast restaurant to get something to eat on the way home. She got in the car and ordered breakfast from the restaurant around the corner from her place. She tried to hurry so that she could catch the afternoon chick flick. Once Kirsten finished her meal, she only made it halfway through a movie about a cheating husband before she had fallen asleep.

Kirsten awoke from her nap on Saturday evening and called her sister to tell her how excited she was about her new job opportunity. She hadn't had the time to tell her sister on Friday, and most likely, she would have to tell the story several times, as everyone in her family would need to hear it for themselves.

"Hey, Aubrey," Kirsten said.

"Hey, what you been up to?" Aubrey replied.

"My usual list of activities, nothing new, except my interview," said Kirsten.

"Oh, yeah, how was that?" asked Aubrey.

"Well, I have a second interview on Tuesday, and you know I always get the job after the second interview," said Kirsten.

"Uh, don't you think you should leave it up to them whether or not you got it?" her big sister asked.

"No, if you leave it up to other people to answer for you, you never get the answer you want," Kirsten replied.

"True, very true! Did you tell Mom, because she is on the other line?" asked Aubrey.

"Tell her you'll call her on three-way; that way I can tell you both at the same time," Kirsten requested.

She told her mom and sister the specifics of her interview, while she thought of how great the job would be. Her mom joined her sister in congratulating, and she was back to watching the movie marathon she had turned to before she had fallen asleep.

Four

A week later, Kirsten had officially accepted her new job in the financial world. She was so excited, and when she learned that she would make almost as much in one week as she made in two at her old job, she flipped. The first thing she did was call her girls. They were great at celebrating, and surely, a new job was a cause for a celebration.

Her first day of work was everything she could have imagined. She walked in and said "Good Morning" to the receptionist, who then, greeted her with a smile, saying "Hi Kirsten, glad to have you!" as she picked up her phone and called the boss of all bosses to the front to meet her. She had never met him before but had heard very much about his work. He was an older guy from the east coast.

Her new director, Ben Gannett, walked out as a fairly plump, grey haired man with a great big smile. He looked so friendly that he couldn't be the shark he was rumored to be. She shook his hand, as he said, "You must be Kirsten; I heard a lot about you, kid." Kirsten wondered what he could have possibly heard. She felt confident in all her interviews but mostly, because she was able to talk easily about the things she was passionate about. Her test scores to get into the company could probably have been much better, but they were average.

Kirsten accepted his compliment by saying, "Mr. Gannett, I hope they were all good things, or at least a fraction of what I have heard about you."

Her director laughed and said, "Please, call me Ben, and I can tell right now you gone be a heck of a lot better than I ever was; you just do what we tell you to do here, and you'll be a success."

Kirsten followed Ben through the office, as he showed her around her new domain. She noticed that, behind the locked glass doors and cubicle walls, the sales department was empty. Ben saw her reaction and began explaining its emptiness and how he hoped that she would be the start of their new corporate culture. He went on and on about how the past director was unqualified and how he let the place go.

Kirsten listened to his stories of the other offices that he turned around and that this office needed to do the same. Ben ended their journey at a small training room where Jim, Ken and Gary congregated to start her training program. A few seconds after Kirsten and Ben walked in, Brad came in, saying "Okay, is everybody ready to get started?" Kirsten nodded unconsciously, as she looked around the room to help refresh her memory as to who was who.

As soon as Ben left, the power in the room shifted. Now, Brad seemed to be the dominant man. Jim and Ken looked just as insignificant as they had when Ben was in the room; only now, they looked relaxed. Gary sat near the back, as if he were there to make sure the boys played nicely. He had an aura of confidence and stability that said he was too important for this, and as soon as Kirsten had run out of things to notice about him, he said, "Well, I will let you all handle the training. Kirsten, let me know if I can help you with anything."

"Okay, thank you," she replied.

Brad looked at the door with a certain look of relief. He stood in front of the room with his balding grey head and said, "If we can get started then?" Then, he looked at Jim and Ken, as to demand attention from them. The OCD that Kirsten had detected from him in their previous meeting had begun to pour out, as he adjusted the laptop for his presentation. Kirsten saw much more than his obsessive habits. The fact that he appeared to read the presentation word for word without even looking at the screen showed that his knowledge was of experience. He finished his presentation about why people need financial services and then, handed the floor to a less confident, extremely nervous looking person. Jim got up to speak, more nervous than he had been in their interviews. He stammered through the history of the company and decided to give some background information on the men in the room. As it turned out, Brad had been in the company for almost twenty years and had been promoted through the ranks several times. Jim had been in the business 4 years, starting in sales. He left after 2 years, for a bank job, and was just now coming back as a manager. And, as for Ken, his personality was completely non-existent. He was so full of arrogance that his smug demeanor hid any shred of humanity that could have been left in him.

Kirsten sat and listened and began think of how she would leave her mark, how she could become as accomplished and as wealthy as the boys' club she had stumbled into.

Once they had finished giving her the morning introduction, the group disbursed to their respective destinations, leaving Jim and Kirsten to have lunch. They went to Ayoki, some fancy Chinese restaurant. Kirsten had her mind set on having lunch alone to get familiar with the office, but she couldn't exactly pass up lunch with her manager on the first day.

They sat at the table, waiting for their food to arrive, when they started picking out fortune cookies for each other. Jim threw one at Kirsten first, initially shocking her, before he smiled and said, "Let's see how fortunate you really are." Kirsten opened her fortune cookie to find the words, *Your efforts will result in much profit.* She knew she was a hard worker, and even though she never really believed in fortune cookies, some things were just meant to be.

She was convinced that she was in the right company at the right time and with the right people. Everyone seemed to be really nice and helpful. Most of the information she was receiving seemed like common sense to her, and she loved what she did. She couldn't think of a better way to empower people than financially.

Her manager opened his fortune cookie to find the words *You are lucky!* Kirsten's manager tossed his fortune to the side and said, "What kind of fortune is that?" They both chuckled, as Kirsten said, "Perhaps we'll work well together, and we both will be very successful by the time my training is over."

"Oh, I'm sure we will. All you have to do is find people to talk to, and you will be okay," said Jim.

"You all were saying that a lot of people don't last, why?" asked Kirsten.

"Well, for different reasons, mostly because they don't try. If you follow the training, it's easy though. You are our only rookie for now, so the more people you put us in front of, the better off you will be," said Jim.

"I thought you have company clients that you will be training me with," asked Kirsten.

"Well, we will. You see, what has to happen before we can put you in front of people you don't know is that you have to be appointed, and that is after your training. So, technically, you can talk to your family and friends before then and have myself, or any of the other managers, sell something to them, and then, we will put it under your name when your training is completed," said Jim.

"Okay, so, how will I know what to sell people if I haven't been trained yet?" asked Kirsten.

Kirsten had a puzzled look on her face. She knew she had to be trained, but the fact that she couldn't sell anything to real people until after the training was kind of weird. She wondered what happened to the hands on stuff and what they said about her having more than enough practice before the time came. Her boss assured her that she would do well, that he would help her be successful.

They completed their meal and headed back towards the office. Kirsten knew her day was only halfway done. She had to complete a portion of the technology training before she could take her laptop home with her, and unfortunately, they spent more time at lunch than they had anticipated.

Once at her desk, Kirsten had begun the web based training and found herself breezing right through it, with the exception of pausing to speak to the experienced agents that would come by, whom she was sure to introduce herself to. She didn't mind taking a break from her training, because most of it, she remembered from her classes in college. Besides, having the 15-20 minute conversations that she had with the other reps could lead to her having a mentor.

She looked forward to finding a mentor and quick; she knew that the sooner, the better. The more help she would have when she needed it, instead of having to wait until she had something to work on and then, start looking. She had been advised that that was the best thing to do. She had also been advised to watch her back, because it was a cut throat business. Talking to the service staff was becoming more training than her computer training assignments; they managed to point out most of the selfish reps who would offer their services just to go on appointments with her to get cuts on her commissions. She was told that they would probably never take her out with them but would make it seem like they wanted to, just to get her working for them.

Kirsten almost couldn't believe that people would stoop so low, but it didn't matter to her anyway. She had several managers saying they were willing to help her, and because they weren't commission employees, they were really just there to help her.

Over the next couple of weeks, Kirsten sat at her computer, pretty much from eight to eight unless she had a lunch meeting or wanted to take a break. She would take breaks and go to the mall to get rid of the effect her computer had on her eyes. The mall was in walking distance from her office; it was through a tunnel, which made it easy for her to get away and practice meeting new people. Not only was everything she wanted practically next door, there were clothes, food and people; all she had to do was go home to shower which was pretty much what she did.

Kirsten enjoyed going to work and learning about investments and insurance and other financial tools that she could advise people on. She never knew people had so many tools to help them maintain or grow wealth. She also loved the fact that she kept meeting people and that her job actually worked best for her in that way. She would go out with her friends and get someone's business card, and it might actually be considered work for her to call and say she enjoyed meeting them. She would even come back to the office and have voicemails from people who wanted to get together for lunch or coffee.

One day, Kirsten received a message from a familiar voice. The man sounded nervous and talked kind of fast, so she replayed it and slowed it down. It said, "Hi Kirsten, this is Josh. I stopped by to see you, and they told me that you had gotten a new job. I hope you don't mind that they gave me the number, but I wanted to take you to lunch." Kirsten saved the message and got the number from the voicemail attendant. She guessed Josh was too nervous to leave his phone number. She didn't plan on calling him right away, but she made the practice of not burning any bridges that she didn't have to burn, including guys that kept reaching for relationships that she didn't want. She stuck his number on a post-it and put it on her board.

The time finally came for Kirsten to use the licenses and the training that she had acquired. She had called everyone who she had spoken to over the last couple of weeks and set appointments.

The first couple of meetings were hard to set, because even though all her managers said they would be available, their schedules still seemed to conflict. Kirsten had decided to go on the appointments anyway, asked lots and lots of questions and even gave some examples of what she could do. Then, she would come back and do her research. After practicing it the first couple of times, she seemed to be quite good at it. She wondered why she needed her managers to go with her in the first place.

Kirsten now found that she had to attend a meeting every morning to update the office on what she had done, how many appointments she had set and also, find out what other people were doing around the state. Some had extremely large cases that paid a ton of money, and others barely made it to the board. They would talk about how they met their clients, how long it had taken to close the sale or to get it through underwriting and compliance and then, any of the hard stuff they had to deal with on the particular case.

Kirsten quickly learned her favorite phrase "quality not quantity" worked in such a different way on her job. For instance, the quality of the product and/or the client didn't matter; it was the amount the client paid for the product that mattered. Also, if she didn't have quality and quantity she would starve. To date, she hadn't seen any of the company leads they promised her she'd have, and when she asked, they'd tell her, "We'll work on that, you just make sure you take one of us with you, and we can get you some bigger sales." Kirsten agreed to start taking them, even though she hadn't seen any of them in action, and she would definitely like to see how to make more money under less stress.

Kirsten took her manager to see a close friend of her aunt. She had never met this woman, and her aunt had given her a good recommendation; all she knew was that her name was Tanner. Once they arrived at the aunt's house, she could see that her boss felt completely uncomfortable, even more so than when he had first met her. He put on half a smile, and after Kirsten introduced them, he said, "Hi! How are you?" Kirsten noticed how he didn't even wait for her to answer his question. He just rushed right in to saying, "So, do you want us to sit? Where do you right the biggest checks?"

Kirsten turned around so fast and looked at him like he was crazy. First of all, he didn't know the woman from Adam and didn't even know what she needed, let alone how much, or if anything. Kirsten attempted to save the meeting by saying, "Well, let's see if we can help with anything, and if you decide you would like to work with us, we can do some research and find out what is best for you." Her aunt's friend consented.

Kirsten attempted to watch her boss run a meeting, but his words just kept offending her client. She was down right embarrassed to be on his team. He tried to go through the sales model that they had taught her, but his intelligence sounded more like arrogance. So, instead of him trying to point out why certain things are helpful to have, he just tried to make her feel bad about not having them. After he asked the woman what kind of retirement plan she had, he had shown his true colors, when he insisted that what she had was insufficient.

The woman had worked for her husband her entire life; she didn't make much of an income and therefore, didn't have much of a plan. Everything that she needed was provided to her and then some. For most people, she had the life of a queen, no worries no debts and if anything were to happen to him, she was well taken care of. To Jim, she was ignorant, and he couldn't understand how she would not make her husband pay her a just wage. He couldn't understand that she worked as his secretary to support him, because she loved him and he took her on nice trips, bought her nice things, paid all of the bills and loved her unconditionally, all of which was enough for her.

Kirsten could understand; she knew many women that worked within family businesses that just wanted something to do with their time, perhaps because she was from a small town herself. When she saw the look of confusion and embarrassment on her clients face, she took control.

"That sounds like a job you could have a lot of fun at; I bet your husband couldn't do it without you," Kirsten said smiling. She was trying to get the lady to know that she understood her and that she wasn't the arrogant, uppity salesperson her boss had been. She was there to help put together a financial plan, and her money was just as green as every one else's.

At this point, it turned in to a real good cop/bad cop situation. Jim opened his mouth one more time, saying "Well, he obviously doesn't appreciate you very much, because he doesn't want to pay you."

Kirsten turned to her boss and said, "No, Jim, I don't think you understand; she doesn't work to make a living. She has one. Her husband takes care of her every need and probably much more. She works to support him and show her appreciation for all that he does for her."

"Mrs. Tanner, I think I have a very good understanding of you and your husband's lifestyle. I, also, have come up with some ideas to help compliment, and maybe, even simplify that lifestyle. If you don't mind, I'd like to take this information and do a little more research on some things. If you could give me a week or so, it may not take that long, but I'll call you so that I can come and show you some options. If you and your husband like those options, we can go from there," said Kirsten.

Jim just sat there with his tail between his legs, because Kirsten was the only thing standing between Mrs. Tanner's foot and his rear end. She gave off a light smile after she heard Kirsten's close and said, "Sure, I would love to have you come back, Kirsten." Kirsten knew that meant not to bring the jittery and arrogant man back into her house.

Kirsten was surprised. All of his so-called experience meant nothing; he obviously didn't understand her clients and wasn't personable enough to try. Kirsten knew she would end up being forced to take him out again, but she would put it off as long as possible. Mrs. Tanner would have been the first of three clients to request that he not accompany her to the next appointment.

As Kirsten advanced in her career, the harder it became to get an answer to anything. It was almost as if she had to stay away from authority to keep her clients, but she needed the help getting either more or bigger accounts to deal with. She was learning that the harder she worked, the more resources she exhausted, but the work wasn't replenishing her resources.

Five

After a few more weeks of work, Kirsten became somewhat addicted to her job; she just kept telling herself, if I work harder, I'll make more. But, working harder just meant that she spent more time thinking about what she should do as opposed to actually knowing what to do. She was flying by the seat of her pants and had no idea what to do about it.

She began to come up with idea after idea for growing her business. Each one she presented, she was told, "We don't have the budget for that" and "You'll have to pay for that expense on your own." Her favorite was "You have to see more people, and then, you'll make more money."

She was fed up. She had established relationship after relationship and had been to company after company, and the fact was that building a business like hers took time. Everyone knew it; everyone said it, but everyone made it seem like she just needed to work harder. None of the people who were so gung-ho to help when she had first gotten there had done a thing, even after she had asked them for advice and tips. Everyone just kept saying, "See more people." "Who could I see?" she thought. She had seen everybody, and none of the people she saw were the people who the company promised they would put her in front of. Here, she was advertising and volunteering in the name of a company who could do only one thing, which was to pat her on the back for her efforts and say "You're a natural at this kid." All Kirsten could think was "If I am such a natural, how come I am broke."

After she had spun all her wheels, Kirsten began to clean off her desk, thinking maybe if I were more organized, I could get more done. She called every post-it and note that she had lying around so that she could throw it away; maybe if they called back, she would make a new one. She had gotten to the one that she wrote for that guy Josh and debated on calling him back.

She dialed the phone, and when he said hello, she said, "Hey, Josh, this is Kirsten. Sorry it took so long to call you back, but I lost your post it note and just found it after cleaning my desk."

"Oh, that means they are keeping you busy over there?" he asked.

"I guess you can say that," Kirsten said, biting back words indicating that they really weren't keeping her much of anything. His saying that had made her feel even more alone in her journey. She began to think that she should just quit, and then, she thought, why should she quit. She had never quit anything that she loved, and she definitely didn't want to keep going from job to job. She would just show them by doing it without their help.

In all of her thoughts, she hadn't even noticed that she was being asked a question, just until he said, "hello are you still there?" She immediately became alert and said, "Oh, yeah, yeah!"

"So, I can pick you up at the office at 12, then?" he replied.

"Huh?" she asked.

"Lunch, at 12?" he repeated.

Kirsten couldn't exactly explain what had just happened, so she accepted the lunch on his terms and decided it might even be good for her to take her mind off her stupid job. She got off the phone with him after exchanging cell phone numbers for the meeting they had just set and then, went on to make the rest of her follow up calls.

After completing her calls, she decided to clean out her email box. She emptied everything that everyone had sent her with meaningless information in it and replied to every email that had been sent just to say hello.

She got down to an email from a girl named Stephani. Stephani's email was more annoying than the regular emails that had meaningless information in it. She sounded presumptuous and so sure of something that she was clueless about.

> *Hi Kirsten,*
>
> *I hope that this letter finds you well. I obtained your email from my cube-mate, Joe. He mentioned to me that he thought we had a lot in common. Perhaps, it is because we are both in a sorority. Or maybe even that you are as ingenious and resourceful as I am. I know that our organizations breed excellence, so I am sure that if he speaks well of you, there must*

be truth to it. In an attempt to remind you of who Joe is, the two of you attended training in New York together; he was the extremely tall, nice guy.

I would very much appreciate a conversation with you; perhaps, we can share some ideas on building our business.

Best Regards,

Stephani

Kirsten thought to herself, who does this chick think she is? Of course, I remember Joe, and I am sure that we don't have that much in common. All sorority girls are not alike, and she definitely sounds nothing like me. Kirsten took a deep breath and replied to 'Stephani's' email; after all, on second thought, she did sound just like her. She was just as excited about the opportunity as Kirsten was when she first started. She was sure to send her regards to Joe and mention that she was rarely in the office, but if she ever left a message or if there was anything Kirsten could do to help, she would. That was her best blowoff e-mail ever, only it didn't work so well.

Stephani called her the next morning, rambling about how great of an opportunity they had. Kirsten thought to herself, this chick must not know what she's in for, or maybe, she actually had an office that could support her, especially since she had cube mates. Kirsten was all by herself; there was no one to understand her, no one to talk to her on her level and no one for her to do business with.

She talked to Stephani, just long enough to affirm her thoughts after the email, and had every intention of not talking to her again. Only Stephani thought it would be a good idea to look at each other's marketing materials, you know, to get ideas. However, Kirsten was a little more experienced than Stephani. She had already learned that the marketing materials they were required to make for the training they had to go through sucked, and there was much more to the job than what they would have her believe. Her short time in the company, she learned that her background was completely different from the older men that she worked with. She knew that she was from a town where people didn't learn about the products she sold, and she had a feeling that Stephani was about to learn the same thing. She shared her work anyway and said that if she had any questions, just ask.

Kirsten left to meet her lunch buddy downstairs in the lobby. He was cuter than she remembered and was dressed much better than she last saw him. Josh was coming from work and had a nervous appearance if she had ever seen one. She shook his hand and smiled, as she said hello to him. His reply was a shy hello and a sappy joke about how bright her smile was.

Kirsten laughed, as she faked a blush and said, "I will have to head in the opposite direction after lunch; do you mind if we go in separate cars?" Kirsten asked.

"Well, where would you like to go?" he asked.

She was kind of irritated that he had asked her to lunch and didn't have any plans. She had always been taught that when you made suggestions or invitations, you should back them up. Kirsten asked if he had anything in mind, and after he said, "not really," she suggested a deli that was across the street.

Kirsten sat across from him and sized him up. He seemed to have a sweet personality. He spoke as if he was from a good family and talked about his activities in the community. They laughed and talked over their food, as if they had known each other for a while.

Josh could carry a conversation well; he asked questions and listened to the answers, and he laughed on cue. He even had a slight charm through all of his nervousness. Kirsten wondered how he could be the same guy that continued to ask her out to watch him play ball, and sure enough, she would ask.

"So, what exactly do you do?" asked Josh, before Kirsten could get her question out.

"I like to say I help people understand financial services. Mostly, my bosses want me to sell investments and insurance. I can do a number of things, and the things I can't, I can put them in touch with others who can."

"Do you like it?" he asked.

"I would actually have to say I do. I would even say I love what I do."

"What do you love about it?"

"Well, the people I meet, the people I actually get to help and learning about the products I sell and how they relate to what other professionals do. There is always something different, you know?"

"How about you? Do you like what you do, besides play basketball?"

He showed a confused look on his face and laughed, saying "You remember that, huh?" Kirsten shook her head yes, as he went on to explain. "Well, I like what I do. We always need a place to live right? But, I do like basketball much better though."

"So, is that where people hang out now, at the basketball court?"

"No, I really don't know what I was thinking."

"Your girlfriend must watch you play?"

"Uhhh, she used to."

"So, why did she stop?"

"Well, I'm glad you asked that because I was trying to figure out how to tell you I had a girlfriend. She is kind of selfish, so I don't really ask her to go anymore."

"If she is selfish, I don't blame her. You want her to watch you play games and not even include her to play with, as if that would really be any better, but to just sit there and watch you?! Who's selfish here?"

Kirsten sat there, thinking why everyone seems to have a hard time saying that they have a relationship with someone. She could care less; she was very relieved that she was limited to interacting with him. Her idea was not to burn any bridges; she didn't exactly say she wanted to build one.

They finished their lunch, as Kirsten said, "It was nice talking with you. I hate to cut it short, but I have to get back to work." She extended her hand to shake his, and he met her with disappointment. He looked as if he wasn't ready to go quite yet. Kirsten left the deli and headed towards the opposite end of town; she had a few potential clients that she wanted to stop and say hi to. Besides, she couldn't think of anything else to do; she had found too many potential clients and not enough actual clients.

Kirsten returned to her office the next day to find that her desk had some unsolicited material on it. As she picked up the material, she saw the words "see me". It was a sales lead. She looked confused when she saw the amount they wanted to purchase and the address she would have to travel to get the sale completed.

Kirsten saw her manager walking past her office space and said, "Jim, you want me to see you about this?"

"Oh, yeah," he said with a grin on his face. "I got you a lead; it's up there in your home town. Do you think you could go there anytime soon? But, since I purchased it, you will have to split it with me 50/50," he continued.

"No, thank you," she said.

"What do you mean, no thank you?"

"Jim, you are giving me a lead that I have to drive two hours to get; the commission won't even cover my gas to get there after it's 'split'. I have to say no, thank you. I think it would be just as good of an idea for you to drive yourself there and keep it," replied Kirsten.

"I figure since you knew the area it would be an experience for you; maybe you will get another sale from it," said Jim.

"If it were about the experience, you would have run the case and taken me along to see how it's done or to close another sale. No offense, but the experience doesn't pay the rent; I can't afford to drive two hours for an experience at this point," said Kirsten.

"Well, Kirsten, you have to understand that the more people you see, the better off you are in this job," said Jim.

"I understand it, really I do. I see people everyday; I meet new people everyday. You said yourself that it's not done overnight. At the same time, when you hired me, I was told that the company would provide more than enough people for me to sell to. I haven't seen it. If things are to continue to go the way they have been going, then you expect me to bring in all the clients and do all the work, and while everyone else is sitting pretty, I am sweating to make numbers," said Kirsten.

"Well, I am on the line, too. I am supposed to go on the appointments with you, and I get I trouble for not being able to account for you. You don't report what you are supposed to report and…"

Kirsten interrupted Jim to say, "I report when I have something to report. If I haven't sold anything, then I have nothing to report."

"Well, report zero, but you need to report something; my name needs to be on at least seven of your appointments," said Jim.

"Well, then, I would be lying, because you don't go on seven appointments with me, and you don't set any for me to go with you. I am sorry; I just don't understand my relationship with the company," said Kirsten.

Actually, she understood the relationship quite well. She worked for a group of people who were in a bad position; their job was to train her, but none of them knew how or maybe, didn't want to. Whatever the case, her job was to bring them business. They had no obligation to her and could care less about her success. She had talked to enough people to know that she was in a bad position, too.

There were two types of rookies, the ones who worked for managers and the ones who worked for agents. The ones who worked for managers struggled to learn and struggled to live. The managers were lucky enough to collect salaries for watching the rookies do what they should be able to teach them to do and collected bonus if the rookies could actually figure it out for themselves. The rookies that worked for agents were trained and taught everything they needed to know and were taken good care of in the process.

Kirsten had held her tongue for a few months too long. She had been trying not to tell her manager that she didn't trust him with her career, but her tongue was getting full. She knew months ago that he didn't stay in sales, because he wasn't very good at it. After seeing him with her clients, she could understand why. She was okay with knowing that she was on her own, but to be on her own and to take shit from people who couldn't do anything for her was getting to be too much.

"Well, Kirsten, you are supposed to make phone calls at night," said Jim.

"I do; it doesn't take that long," she replied.

"You could do 'lunch-n-learns' to see more people," Jim suggested.

"I can barely buy myself lunch. Buying it for 20 others is not going to work."

"Order pizza or sandwiches," Jim said.

"Okay, you don't understand. Lunch isn't an option," said Kirsten.

"Are you calling 150 people a week?"

"Well, who do you suggest I call?"

"Whoever you want to call."

"I don't know 150 more people; do you?"

"No, but you can call a list of businesses."

Kirsten listened and tried to maintain her composure. She knew that they were getting nowhere. He wasn't willing to acknowledge the problem, and she didn't know any other way to point it out.

"Maybe you could show me; you did say that this is what you used to do right?" She knew he would try his best, because he was actually a decent person. So, he did.

Kirsten sat across from Jim, as he received her response of no, no, no and another no to everything he suggested. Then, he said, "Well, that's just how it is; sometimes you get lucky."

Kirsten could care less about luck; she wanted success. She knew she was smart enough and ambitious enough to do it. "Well, thanks for trying," she said.

She walked out of his office to her own work space and grabbed her belongings to head for the elevators. She needed to get out of the stifling air that she had been sitting in since the morning. “I can do nothing at home in my own comfort,” she said to herself.

Heading down the elevators to the main entrance, she thought to herself, Numbers Game! They keep telling me to talk to people, see people, and call your family and friends. How long do they want me to try this before I fail? Where can I see a lot of people at once, for free? Kirsten sat in the driver’s seat of her car and pulled out her cell phone. She called everyone she knew in HR and everyone in management; she left a ton of messages and even got some people to check to see what they could do. She needed to tell as many people as possible what she could do for them.

She remembered her friend, Camron and realized that she hadn’t contacted him since her change in jobs. She called him to let him know about her move in hopes to solicit his help for her new plans

“Hey, Camron, how are you?” she said.

“I am just fine, yourself?”

“Great, this is Kirsten; we met a little while back at the wine bar.”

“Oh, hey! I tried to call you, but you moved jobs.”

“Yeah, I did. You know, we all have to grow in life, right.”

“Sure do, so what are you doing now?”

“Insurance and investments.”

"For real? That's nice. We have an intern right now doing some research on it. Yeah, we're trying to get people to help them understand their finances and options a little better, you know?"

"Yeah, I know exactly what you mean; maybe, I could talk to her. I am sure I can serve as a shortcut for her. I could also come and set up a table to talk to people who want help with that kind of thing."

"Okay, that would work out well; you might even get some business out of it. Let's get together for lunch and talk about it," said Camron.

Kirsten ended her conversation with Camron and yelled, "Yes!" once she hung up the phone. "All I need is a few more of those, and I would be set." She focused her mind back on other opportunities to help her grow her business. What else, what else? she said aloud to herself.

Kirsten got out of her car and walked swiftly into her apartment. Her energy level was high, and the adrenaline built, as she tapped her fingers on her coffee table, trying to think. Okay, it's only 3:00; what else can I do today? Then, Kirsten's phone rang with a familiar number.

"Hello, this is Kirsten," she said.

"Kirsten, this is Tom; I got your message. Good to hear from you," he said.

"Yeah, it's nice to speak with you again, too."

"So, what can I do for you," said Tom.

"I called, because I do insurance and investment products now. I would like to come and host a fair for your employees, so they can learn and talk to me about the products and services they may need, supplemental to what you offer."

"Well, you know, Kirsten, I know you're a great person. I would love to help you out, but I am limited by our current providers as to who I can let in the door," said Tom.

"I see," said Kirsten.

"Hey, look, we are reviewing the companies we deal with to see who offers the better platform. If you could get some information on the platforms you offer, perhaps you can be one of the companies we use. Then, you can talk to whoever you want."

"Okay, Tom, I will see what I can do. Thanks," said Kirsten.

"Hey, anytime, just let me know how I can help."

Kirsten hung up the phone with better news than she had expected. Having a corporate account would do her much better than a few accounts from sitting at a table. She sat on the couch, trying to get a grip on what she was doing. Her adrenaline was so high that she found herself shaking her legs uncontrollably.

She pulled out her laptop to see what she could find on corporate accounts and kept coming up blank. She could always wait until the next day at work, but she had her mind set on finding the answer as soon as possible. She looked for another two, until she just didn't have any place else to search for the information.

Kirsten poured herself a glass of Cabernet to relax. It was night, and she knew if she didn't go to sleep soon she wouldn't be able to. She sipped her wine and watched the rerun episodes from her childhood shows. Soon, after her glass of wine was gone, she was asleep and dreaming.

Kirsten's eyelids jumped as she slept. She saw herself in a struggle with her three adversaries on the stairs. This one was a struggle unlike anyone she had experienced. She no longer had an innocent, leave me alone demeanor. She was fighting tooth and nail for her life, but they, on the other hand, were just casually playing around with her, which made her angrier. They held her arms and sat on her, as if they were playing. The one man was standing around playing with the knife she had seen before, but she still felt threatened.

Kirsten thought, "This isn't a game; you don't play with knives." She saw her mouth moving, as she would grit her teeth and try to scream, "leave me alone." She struggled with them a few minutes longer, until someone dropped the knife in her. Kirsten yanked herself from her sleep and woke up sweaty with achy muscles and teary eyes. She felt as though she had just fought a war.

She knew that she had just had the same bad dream she had been having, but she couldn't understand why. Who was she fighting? Why were they after her? Why the heck was she even having these dreams? Kirsten got up from her attempted rest and walked to her bathroom. She definitely needed to calm herself down, and going back to sleep in a hot sweat wasn't in her plans. She turned on the hot water and walked into it slowly, until it no longer burned her caramel colored skin. "God, what am I doing?"

Six

Kirsten went into the office with her hopes high and her head held even higher. She'd been trying really hard not to let the people around her know that her career choice was depressing her in such a way. At times, her head may have been a little too high from overcompensation, but today, it was just right. Today, she actually had good reasoning for her pride.

She walked into her morning meeting and sat, waiting for her turn to speak. "I set three appointments, earned $700 in commissions and I have two appointments for today," said someone on the conference line. Kirsten listened, as they went one after another, listing their accomplishments or lack thereof. She heard the usual number of expected successes and the even more abundant failures from the mediocre few like herself. She listened to the numbers, as she thought to herself that someone had to be trying hard to ignore the trend in success rates; she also hoped that she could break that trend.

"Kirsten… Kirsten?" Jim called.

"Uh, yes."

"It's your turn," said Jim.

"Oh, I set four appointments; I earned $300 in commissions, and I have one of those appointments set for today.

"Okay, so tell us about the other three," said Jim.

"A retiree from the fire department, the benefits guy from Emarby National, and an intern at The Uniform People," said Kirsten.

"You have two companies in there; those are really good grounds for referrals," said Jim.

"Actually, Emarby is redoing their benefits, and perhaps, I could get the whole company, and The Uniform People are letting me set up shop," said Kirsten.

"Oh, well, you can't do a corporate account; you will just turn it over to someone in group accounts, and you will have done all that work for nothing," said Jim.

"There is still an opportunity if I have to do it that way," said Kirsten.

"What kind?…well, we can talk about this later. Everybody, thanks for calling in. The meeting is adjourned," said Jim.

Kirsten sat and waited for all to dismiss themselves before she started talking. "I don't understand why I can't take a corporate account?" said Kirsten, trying her best not to sound like a brat.

"Well, we have a department within the company that does that, so they would take it over, having wasted your time," said Jim.

"That just doesn't sound right," said Kirsten.

"Okay. I'll ask Brad to be sure. But, for now, I need you to check with compliance on the last few cases you did," said Jim.

Kirsten went off with a deflated disposition for the time. She knew there was a chance that she could do a corporate account, but if she could, there was no one to show her how to do it. Surely, it wasn't in any of her training manuals. She sat at her desk, sorting through all of the emails that she could. Each one resulting in a blind trail of bureaucracy, where she had to send a request for someone else to make a request, for someone else to do a job and someone else to follow up on it and then, finally, report their findings back to her.

Kirsten had never chased money so much; she had always chased life, but her career forced her into the position where money had become everything. She couldn't do her job without having money, and she couldn't make any money unless she had it. She had tried her best to market herself as a resource for people, but not even putting fliers in mailboxes at 4 a.m. had brought her any business.

After not being able to do her corporate account anytime soon, she knew that she needed something else to bring her money immediately. She took a break from her email tasks and went to the career finder's web page. She was searching for a 3rd shift job that would pay her bills, while she figured out how to expand her business.

She loved her job wholeheartedly and couldn't accept the idea of failing, because someone else wasn't capable of doing their job. She felt bad saying that her situation was someone else's responsibility, but she didn't know what else to say. She had expounded every possible resource and was still coming up short. Calling herself incompetent was getting old, and she realized the only thing she could be faulted for was riding it out.

She found a website that hosted 3rd shift job postings and searched for their phone number. Once she called them, she lined up a job starting the next day, paying only half of what she was supposed to make for her quota per week. Since she hadn't been making her quota, she thought she might as well take it.

The next day, Kirsten finished her assignments at the office and went to grab some quick food before starting her next job. On her way to work, she called her distant co-worker, Stephani to make sure she had been making strides in her job. Kirsten was still baffled as to how she could go from not wanting to be bothered by Stephani to wanting to protect her from the things she, herself, was experiencing.

"Hey, Steph, are you busy?" asked Kirsten.

"Kind of, I am walking into a meeting with a client," replied Stephani.

"Yeah! That's good. Sell something," said Kirsten.

"Okay, I will. Can I call you back in like, two hours?" asked Stephani.

"No, sorry. This might be the last time you talk to me for the next three days. I am working night shifts, but

I'm off for the following three days after that," said Kirsten.

"Dang, Kirsten, three days straight! When will you sleep?"

"I won't this week, but maybe next," Kirsten responded jokingly.

"Okay, well, have fun; glad I'm not you," said Stephanie.

"Well, Steph, sell something, so you won't have to be."

"Okay, seriously, you know you don't have to work two jobs; you can just go to a bank. Hell, you could go anywhere. You are just too stubborn to."

"That's not the point. I don't want any bank job; I want to stay with my clients. If I leave them, I can't get them back for two years; not only that, I am not letting this company get the best of me. I can do the job just as good as anybody in the 'boys' club'. Anyway, go sell something. I am sure we will catch up later. Bye."

"Okay, Bye!"

Kirsten finished her food and walked into the door marked employees only. She didn't know much about working in a factory, other than her degree qualifying her to manage one. What she did know was that she needed to maintain her lifestyle, while she figured out how to make her actual career work for her. If this was the way she had to do it, then it was as good as done.

She reported to the office, and a man walked by, saying "Your shift doesn't start for ten minutes. You have to go to the break room; until then, you can't be here." Kirsten looked around to see where the break room was and before she could ask him, he had put in his earplugs and walked away.

Kirsten walked around, looking for the break room she had been directed to and eventually found it just before her shift. She sat in on what sounded like a pep talk, only there wasn't much pep, and half of the room seemed to be preoccupied with head phones or newspapers. When the guy talking had dismissed everybody, Kirsten addressed him, saying "Excuse me, I'm Kirsten; I'm supposed to start today." "Okay, give me a sec; I'll find out where you go," he said.

"Okay, and what's your name? asked Kirsten.

"Oh, I'm Ryan, the floor super."

He walked out of the break room, and Kirsten sat there for almost fifteen minutes before anyone returned to give her instructions. Ryan walked back in and said, "You are going to pack at machine 15; just go down the middle aisle and make sure there are 50 parts in each box. If you need any help, just come and find me."

"Okay." said Kirsten

She found the machine he had sent her to, and she spent the next couple of hours packing boxes. She almost liked her new job. She didn't have to worry about anything, and no matter what, she would be paid when the work was done.

By 12 midnight, Kirsten was good and ready for lunch and couldn't wait to see what she had missed, since she had been inside the factory. No sooner than she had sat down to eat and check her phone, she was receiving a phone call from an unknown number.

"Hello?' she said.

"Hey, Kirsten, this is Josh."

"Uhm, hi… can I help you with something?"

"Yeah, uh, I was just thinking about you, and I wanted to call and see what you had been up to."

"It's like, midnight; I would prefer that you not call me so late." Kirsten was thinking to herself that she would prefer him not to call her at all, especially if he thought it was okay to call so late.

"Oh, I'm sorry; were you sleeping?" asked Josh.

"I don't think that matters, but yeah, I usually am at this time," replied Kirsten.

"Okay, I'll try you some other time," said Josh.

"Okay, bye, but can you be sure to not call me so late?"

"Okay, bye, sweet dreams."

Did this dude just wish me sweet dreams? How creepy is that? she thought to herself. Kirsten checked the rest of her calls and noticed that she had missed two other calls from the same number. She was irritated that he had called her so late and so frequently. She hated when she was younger, and her mom wouldn't let her use the phone after 11:00 p.m. Now, she knew why. She didn't know why this Josh dude was so hard pressed to talk to her, but she wasn't interested. She also had an earlier call from her new friend, Camron, who followed up with a text message, saying "Called you, guess you were busy; let's do lunch tomorrow." She saved the message so that she could remember to call and make arrangements with him and headed back to work.

She worked the rest of the night at the same station she had before, and at 7 a.m., she was free to go. Much like she expected, her body felt so tired and sleepy, but unfortunately for her, she had a meeting to get to in two hours.

Kirsten drove her twenty minutes home to take an hour nap and got ready in another twenty. All she had to do was make it to the office before her meeting started, and she could get on with her day.

"Kirsten!" her boss called.

"Kirsten, are you listening to me?"

"Yes, I heard you."

"Well, you just didn't look like you were paying attention."

She was sitting in the meeting for two hours, barely functioning and trying to hide her fatigue. She really wasn't listening; she knew the sales model he was pitching like the back of her hand. She also knew that it only worked on uneducated suckers who wanted to flex how much money they had or wished they had. She kept thinking back to the meetings he had gone to with her and trying to figure out how in the world he had been so lucky.

She now felt lucky that he ended his presentation and dismissed the meeting. She headed straight for the lounge and poured herself some coffee to help get her work done and then, went through her emails and phone calls before she could go to lunch.

"Hi, may I speak with Camron please?" asked Kirsten.

"Speaking," he said.

"Camron, it's Kirsten; I just got your message about lunch. Still want to go?" she asked.

"Sure, let's meet at that new grill up there. Can you meet me in half an hour," he replied.

"Perfect, I'll see you then," Kirsten agreed.

Kirsten hung up the phone and packed her computer and the things she needed to get back to her normal life and day job, so she didn't have to go back to the office after lunch. She then headed out the door for her meeting and was so excited that she had the weekend off. Her half day in the office felt like forever. Her plans were to go to lunch, and then, she could go home and sleep until church on Sunday.

Climbing out of her car, she noticed Camron smiling and walking towards her. She smiled back at him when he spoke, saying "Hello Miss Kirsten, how are you today?" "Just fine and yourself?" she replied. By the time he answered, saying "I'm doing well, thanks," he was opening the door for her to walk in. He was a lot shorter than she remembered him being, but at least he was a gentleman, which seemed to be a hard thing to find, especially in the men that she worked with.

They talked about each other's career paths and how they had gotten to places they were in life. Then, Camron said, "I know you were thinking of coming to my company and doing some presentations. We also talked about you hosting an informational. What I would like to do is have you come in for a day and set up in our lounge; it's fairly large. You will have plenty of people to talk to, but you would have to have that meeting with the intern, simply because we are a union plant, and there will be some things you can't talk about."

"Sounds fine; I have already talked with her about the logistics, so all we need is a time and date," said Kirsten.

"Great! I will let you arrange that with her, and we can go back to talking about other stuff," said Camron.

They sat for nearly an hour and a half, eating and talking and trying to get to know each other. Kirsten couldn't help but think about how nice he was and how well he communicated, how well they communicated together. They had some of the same interests and many of the same hobbies. They ended their meeting with another one scheduled for the following week, and Kirsten was off to hibernate.

Nearly months had passed since Kirsten's ideas were launched. She had gone to The Uniform People and talked to many individuals who wanted to be contacted, but somehow, the business never came quick enough. She couldn't afford to chase the people who just didn't want to close the sale nor did she have the energy. She kept telling herself that her job couldn't be this hard, but she was exhausted.

As time passed, she had learned that she could have actually done her big corporate account; only now, she had missed the company's deadline, which also meant she missed out on a big commission. She couldn't help but think that if she hadn't spent so much time at her other job or hanging out with Camron, she could have gotten on top of things.

She also learned that the relationship she and Mr. Camron had been developing was a bust. He was married which meant he was now on her list of people to stay away from. It was quite a pity, too; he seemed to be of a dying breed. He was well groomed, smart and had his life on track. He insisted that he was soon to be divorced, but Kirsten just couldn't get over the fact that he had withheld being married in the first place

The icing that topped the cake for her was hearing that having her second job was against her contract, so now, she really had to work harder if she wanted to survive in her business. Still, nothing seemed to be going her way except trouble, and that seemed to be easy to find.

Seven

Kirsten couldn't help but think that, with history repeating itself, all of the answers to life's issues would be figured out by now, but her problems were just beginning. As she took her two hour drive to her parents' home in the suburbs from her big city apartment, she wrapped her mind around having to ask her dad for help. Though he always said, "You gonna live in this world, and you ain't gonna live in it by yourself," she always had to prove that she could if she had to.

Kirsten had gotten some practice talking about bad jobs, especially after the job with the meat man. Her mind flashed back to how she had put herself in such a compromising position, but no one could have predicted that. This time, her father had given her fair warning, and she didn't listen. Now, she had to figure out what to tell him. She thought to herself that she could just tell the truth. After all, this was her dad and dads love to take care of their little girls. She, now needed to figure out how to word the truth, which was that she was a grown ass woman, who couldn't support herself. Only, she knew the first thing her dad would say is "See, I told you not to take that job; see, you hard-headed," and she would end up having to defend herself, which was something she hated to have to do, especially to her dad. Her daddy was a genius; he could do no wrong in her eyes, and that was a legacy that was hard for her to live up to.

Most everything Kirsten did was to impress her daddy; in turn, she tried to keep all of her mistakes from him, which usually ended up making her work harder than she had to, which brought her back to trying to figure the best way to break the news. She couldn't exactly smile and say, guess what daddy? I have to quit my job, because I'm not making enough money, so I'll have to move back home with you and mom. Oh and, by the way, I'd be breaking my lease which would cost me more money. What do you think?

Her own sarcasm annoyed her to no end, and as usual, when she had sarcastic conversations with herself, it was because she had no idea as to what she could have done to have made her plans come out better and no indication as to what was next, so she was stuck in her own miserable situation.

Kirsten was relieved that it was Thursday evening, which meant that after her moment of truth with her parents, they'd all go to sleep; she'd work Friday and then, visit friends later that night. So, she'd only be home for a few hours in the afternoon, and by the time everyone settled in on Saturday, it'd be time for her to leave.

As Kirsten pulled up to her parents' home, she began to get into character. She reached into the center console of her car to pull out the aloe wipes that were stashed there. Her car was equipped with everything. She spent so much time away from home she had almost everything she needed on four wheels, from bottled drinks and snack foods to office supplies and even toiletries.

The wet aloe wipes were to give her face a fresh look from the red eyes she was wearing, which said, *I have something I should tell you.* She didn't think she had to tell them everything as soon as she walked in. She continued to get her mind together for the visit to her parents, clearing her throat to make sure she didn't sound too unhappy and practiced greeting her parents. To be completely honest, she loved them dearly and thought they were the best parents ever. To show them, she adapted a way to greet her parents that made them feel special and missed; each time she would say hello to them it was usually in an overly dramatic flattering gesture. Kirsten already had a high voice and her personality was perfect to be able to pull off the dramatic greeting. She had always been extremely energetic and had a colorful thought process, so her parents often teased her about being a politician, when she would say flattering things or dance around questions.

She walked to the door and put on her happy face for her dad in case he was home; then, she attempted to assume an impeccable posture. This was her usual routine for coming home. Her dad always seemed so happy when he thought that his little girl was happy. She could hardly ever pout or cry, because she hated the way her father would look at her when she did. Her mom had always encouraged good posture; being a former dancer, posture meant a great deal to Kirsten's mom. Her mom had always seemed disappointed that her little girl left dance for sports, so she tried not to remind her. Simply put, Kirsten never wanted to be in anybody's shadow. So, when people began to tell her that she moved just like her mother, even if it was meant to be a compliment, it drove her crazy. She wanted her own hobbies, her own fun and didn't need approval to go find it.

Kirsten took her final deep breath before sticking her key into the door. "Please let there be no one home," she mumbled under her breath. As she opened the door, she saw her mother's work bag sitting on the landing of the stair; she knew she was out of luck. "Hello, my Mother!" she said, while forming a cheshire grin on her face. "Hello, my Daughter!" her mother mimicked. They followed there usual routine, kissing both cheeks, as if they were foreigners. Usually, the second kiss was cut short because of the colossal hug her mom would give her.

As Kirsten bent down to pick up the keys that she'd dropped, she saw her little brother, Austin walking down the stairs.

"Hey, baby brother, you love me?" said Kirsten.

"Yeah, but you can get your own crap out of the car…" he replied to her question.

Austin was eighteen, but even though he had grown up, he would always be her baby brother. They looked just alike, once upon a time, until his face grew into the muscles he had developed when he became addicted to football. He was good, but he was better at baseball. When he played, he looked like a natural. Much like Kirsten and her mom, Austin didn't want to be in his daddy's footsteps, so despite his natural gift for baseball, he picked football once he'd gotten into high school. After he started conditioning for the team, he never stopped; he lifted weights like it was just as important as using the bathroom.

"Please," she whined again.

"Aight, man, just give me the keys?" he said.

Kirsten threw him the keys with a smile and then went on to ask, "Where's my daddy?"

Even though she already knew the answer, her mom replied, "I don't know; maybe he'll be home in a few. I think he may have gone to one of his houses." Kirsten's dad had been doing real estate investments for as long as she could remember, and if he wasn't doing his job as a police officer, he was working on one of his houses.

Kirsten had only been home for a matter of minutes. She began to remember how great it was to visit her family. Their home always felt warm and smelled like whatever candle or oil her mom was into at the time.

She walked around too see what had changed since the last time and just long enough to be annoyed. Kirsten, like every young adult, had things she hated about going home; this time, her 'thing' was hard to hide. "Ma… I can't believe you put these pictures in a photo album for all to see; James and I haven't been together in 4 years, and I know it wasn't there the last time I came home." Kirsten was irate; the picture sitting in the family room was of her, sitting on James' lap, hugging his neck from the side. She thought that, clearly, her mom should understand that she kicked him out of the family, and so should she.

As her mom giggled, Kirsten retorted, "That is so not funny! I can't believe it! What if I had brought someone home, and this album was laying here?"

"Oh, Kirsten, get a grip. It's a photo album. That's what people do with them; they archive memories. It has nothing to do with whether or not you are together now. Would you just tell me what you want to eat?" Kirsten's mom asked.

Kirsten, being already in a feisty mood from seeing the pictures of her first love, smarted off at her mom, saying "It's almost 8:00 p.m.; I thought you would have already eaten. Remember the whole thing about not eating after 6 p.m.? And, I know it's not about whether or not we are together now, but if I just walk in and see them.... never mind, I'll just switch it with Aubrey and Devin's album."

"Kirsten, just turn the page and relax; the book isn't just about you and him. And, I waited for you to make a decision on dinner. You know the guys don't eat real food, at least not here. Just tell me what you want," her mom said.

I'm not really hungry; I don't care," Kirsten said after she smacked her lips.

"Kirsten, watch who you are talking to. You might be grown, but this is still my house. We haven't eaten, so what would you like?' her mom said again.

It never failed for Kirsten's mom to ask what was for dinner whenever one of her daughters came home. She had always been one of the greatest hostesses Kirsten had known. She was always very hospitable and accommodating to some reasonable extent. Now that she saw her daughters so infrequently, seeing them was a breeze of fresh air from the men she shared a home with. It didn't change the fact that Kirsten had always hated answering questions about what they should do as a group. She learned growing up that there was no point in putting a bid in on something you could care less about. Each time she would take a guess, someone else would whine about something different that they really wanted. The same even held true as an adult.

"You know, I don't care; you ask that every time I come home. It's either going to be Chinese, Greek or pizza, because you aren't going to cook at 8 p.m., and if you were, it would be chicken with some vegetable medley type thing," Kirsten said.

Kirsten's mom was finding her irritability extremely funny but was growing tired of it. She looked at her youngest daughter and raised her hands as to say, "Whatever! Just pick something."

Kirsten yelled for her little brother, and when her mom asked "Why can't you just pick something?" while shaking her head. Kirsten's thought pattern was to skip a few steps. She knew he would be the designated errand boy, so she'd just ask where he felt like going. By the time Austin had come down the stairs, Kirsten realized that, in a matter of minutes, things had gotten on her nerves at home; it would only get worse the rest of her stay. Therefore, she thought she should tag along with Austin, so she could stop at her favorite place to get drink.

To Kirsten's surprise, her little brother already knew what she called him for; he seemed to be good at that lately. He walked into the kitchen, where Kirsten and his mom were sitting, with Kirsten's keys in hand, saying "Wherever you want me to go I'm taking your car." Kirsten looked at him as though she was shocked, and actually, she was. She tried to make a habit of not leaving her keys around him, so the fact that he dangled them, as he spoke his intentions, left her in awe.

Kirsten walked towards the door, saying "let's go," leaving her mom wondering what they had actually decided on. "Oh, we're getting pizza," said Kirsten. She left, trying to keep up with her overly excited, little brother.

Once in the car, Kirsten said, "I need to stop at Evan's gallery." Evan was an old friend from college, who she'd helped to write the business plan for his wine gallery; she'd even done so much as to convince him to make it a wine gallery as opposed to a liquor store. She hated the idea of placing yet another liquor store into society, but at least if it had to be done, it should be done in class.

Evan's was right across the street from the pizza place, which gave Kirsten just enough time for her stop before the pizza was done.

Austin pulled into the lot, and Kirsten immediately noticed Evans's car. He'd had it for years and had no intentions on letting it go. He drove a Corvette; she couldn't remember what year he bragged about it being, but it was old. He had painted it black with metallic stripes. As laid back as he was, he poured so much of his heart into his car. He had designed the interior himself and if he were mechanically inclined, would probably do the maintenance himself, too. Kirsten almost hated that he loved his car more than anything else, and as she walked into the store, her memory started to replay flashbacks of how she'd met Evan.

As she walked through the door, her friend, Stephani was calling her cell phone. They talked often, but more recently, it had just been recaps on everything that went on when they weren't talking and then, a quick good-bye. Kirsten was lucky the phone rang, because it stopped her from biting her upper lip, which was a trait she had gotten from her dad. It meant she was uncertain about something, and no matter how hard she tried, she couldn't kick the habit of doing it.

"Hey, Steph," said Kirsten.

"Hey, are you busy?"

"No, I'm in the store."

"Oh, wow! I know you don't go to the regular store. I just wish you would take your AA meetings as serious as your 'grocery shopping'," Stephani said laughing.

"Shut Up! You know I don't qualify for AA," said Kirsten

"Keep drinking, and you probably will," joked Stephanie.

"Yeah, right. Anyway, I guess I will have to talk with you later. I can't really hold the bottles and the phone. Bye…hey, remind me to tell you about my trip later," said Kirsten.

"Okay, bye.

"I see you are still biting that lip!" Kirsten heard Evan's voice behind her. Her lips moved as if she had just mouthed the word "shit". Kirsten turned on the charm, and as she turned around to reply, she said, "Hello to you, too!" Her eyes went from the bottom to the top, as she noticed the tip of his loafers underneath his loose fitting jeans, topped with a thick, brown belt and oversized buckle. By the time she got to his brown shirt and the muscles showing underneath it, her expression changed from charming to flirty. There was something about him that sucked her in every time; no matter how hard she worked to forget their relationship, seeing him or hearing his voice would throw everything out the window.

"Hey, Miss Lady," said Evan.

"Hey, what are you doing out front? The owner is just supposed to give direction. You might need to hire some help," Kirsten said.

"Well, maybe you should come help me?" he replied.

"You know I can't move back to this town," said Kirsten.

"Oh, yeah, I forgot; you have to take over the world first," he said, mocking her.

"Whatever! Just point me towards the Vodka, please," Kirsten snapped at him.

"Since when did you start drinking vodka? I thought you were a girly drinker. What happened to the wine and mixed drinks?" Evan asked.

"Don't worry; I'll mix it with a lime, and I'll chase it with cabernet. Thanks!" said Kirsten.

"You still got that sarcasm thing going for you, huh?" Evan retorted.

The tension between the two was growing, as it usually did. A conversation between the two of them was like a competition to see who could get the other to crack first. Both knew they still had feelings for each other, and as hard as they tried to fight it, it showed. Kirsten grabbed her bag to leave when Evan asked, “When can I come see you again?” Kirsten smiled at him and said, “Take care.”

She hated that she couldn’t accept his invitation, but it was obvious that they wanted different things in life and if she had, they definitely wouldn’t remain just friends. After realizing that her little brother went inside for the pizza, she sat her bag on top of the car to reach for her cell phone. It was the perfect time for her to call her friend, Jada, so she could debrief her on her latest contact with their old friend.

Unfortunately, Jada never answered her phone, and that left Kirsten thinking about how she’d met that particular ex.

Eight

Jada had introduced Kirsten to Evan in college. It's even a miracle that they ended up being friends let alone dating. She had been dating her high school sweetheart, James, for three years. So, as a sophomore in college, she was heartbroken to find out that her long distance relationship was ending.

Her first love, James had been M.I.A. for the past couple of months, and when ever she'd try to see him, he would have better things to do. She spent first semester of her sophomore year being miserable, until she finally decided to let him go. After a month of begging and pleading from James, Kirsten finally decided to take him back, days before finding out that he had a baby on the way. Some chick was three months pregnant and not only that, she was pregnant, and everyone knew they had been messing around, except Kirsten.

She was so heartbroken when she found out, and the way she discovered the news didn't make her feel any better. She was in her room when an old friend called her to ask, "Girl, why didn't you tell me what happened?" Kirsten had no idea what she was talking about, but sure enough, her friend would tell her and after finding out that she was involved in drama that she knew nothing about, any chance she and James had was gone. Kirsten could remember, vividly, the way she fell back into her seat. Calmly, the words, "We aren't together anymore, so I really don't care" poured out of her mouth just before she hung up the phone and burst into tears.

She was embarrassed that her boyfriend could treat her so badly after she gave him everything she had. She hated him for it and would pass the blame on to every other man that she would come in contact with. So, when Kirsten met Evan, she was in quite a shitty mood.

Jada had taken Kirsten to her favorite 'Bar & Grill'; in a college town, there wasn't much else to do. Jada was celebrating the news that she had gotten accepted into law school, and Kirsten was just happy to not be in the house. Little did they know, Evan was the new bartender at the place. Evan had asked about Kirsten on several occasions, but he was always told she had a boyfriend. The only thing he cared about was that he was attracted to her and that she seemed to be a nice girl.

Soon after entering the bar, the girls were giving Evan their drink orders, when he said to Kirsten, "You should smile more!" and winked his eye. Kirsten almost took offense to his statement, so after a stern look, she flashed a smile, saying "Thanks, but I smile enough."

Evan shrugged his shoulders, as to concur with Kirsten, when Jada said, "we'll be sitting over there." She grabbed Kirsten by the arm, saying "What's wrong with you? I know you aren't still crappy about your ex; that was a month ago…"

"I know, but all guys are the same. I'm sure he's a jerk, just like the rest of them, and even if he isn't, it wouldn't matter, because I'd still think he had potential to be. So, let's just do what we came here to do, and it wasn't to talk to him. *Cheers*!" Kirsten replied, as she held up her glass.

"You are sick…cheers…," Jada said, reaching over to touch Kirsten's glass.

As the girls sat waiting for a server, they sipped their drinks. They began to laugh about all of the fun stuff they had done and planned to do when they would visit each other.

As Jada talked, she looked over Kirsten's shoulder to see that there was a waiter coming behind her. He was holding a platter covered with what looked like every appetizer they sold. As he put the tray down, both girls said, "We didn't order yet," simultaneously.

The waiter replied, "Hey, look, this is from Evan, so I hope you enjoy."

As Jada smiled, Kirsten said, "We can't take this."

The waiter threw his hands up, saying "It's already been paid for, and I have already been tipped. Besides, if you don't eat it, it gets trashed."

"Thanks, we'll take it," Jada chimed in.

The waiter left just in enough time for the two girls to turn and see Evan nod his head with a smile. That was the last they saw of him that night. They sat and hung out until the crowd came in.

Kirsten ignored Evan, just as she did the other guys she encountered at that point in her life. The difference with him was that he didn't care about whether she would date him; he genuinely wanted to get to know her. He was such a cool guy it got harder for her to ignore him. He gave her the attention she was missing and made her feel comfortable taking it.

Kirsten actually started to think of Evan as a friend after hanging out with him the entire second semester. Needless to say, they became more than friends. By the end of the year, they were lovers. Sometimes, Kirsten wished they had…

"Aight, you ready to go?" Austin said, as he walked toward the car, interrupting her thoughts.

"Yeah, let's go," said Kirsten.

The siblings headed home with their family's dinner and Kirsten's sedative for the weekend. She thought to herself that maybe she'd be able to talk to her parents after dinner. Unfortunately, she couldn't put her mind towards what she should say; it was clouded with everything she didn't want to say.

Austin pulled the car into Kirsten's usual spot when she would visit home. He parked off to the side so that no one blocked her in if she had intentions of leaving, nor could anyone be blocked in, who had intentions on leaving extremely early in the morning.

Her family learned the last couple of times she had visited them not to wake her. She had been so stressed lately that she hadn't been sleeping, so the time she spent at home offered her a certain degree of comfort. She would sit in the guest room that she so desperately tried to claim as her own. She had done the decorating and even visited the most of any guest, but still she knew it didn't belong to her. As long as she lay there, in that bed, in that house she was taken care of. Her family may have had their differences, but the older they got, the less it seemed to matter.

Kirsten never learned how to discuss things that bothered her, which was fine with her, because they never bothered her long. She would look past all that she could; she looked past a lot, because there was always something new that would make her happy again. At this point in her life, she was finally learning to deal with things, because it had been so long since anything new had come along that would make her smile and all else seemed hopeless.

As the brother and sister duo got out of the car, Kirsten's daddy pulled up. They met at the door with half of a hug, minus her usual run and jump, due to her holding the pizza.

"Hey, Daddy," said Kirsten.

"Hey, baby girl, what you doing home?" said her daddy.

"I'm working, Daddy!" she said, in her high-pitched voice.

"Junior, you staying out of trouble?" the Senior Austin asked his son.

"Yes, sir," he answered in a deep voice with his chin up. His dad had always taught him how to talk like a man, so to his father, he spoke with authority and respect. Everyone else got a low deep voice and a lack of expression. The family was okay with that though, because the older he got, the more charm they saw in him. He had more common sense than they had ever given him credit for as a child, and he was more thoughtful and caring than they ever thought the baby boy could turn out to be.

Kirsten walked in with her daddy and went to set the food down in the kitchen. She still wasn't ready to tell him what was bothering her, so she kept her smile on and fixed her parents a plate of pizza and salad, which her mom required them all to eat.

"Kim, you know your daughter was coming home?" Kirsten's dad asked her mom.

She didn't answer him; she just said, "Oh, Austin, don't start wit that girl." She hated that he always pretended someone was keeping something from him. Truth was, it was his way to spark conversation and to tease his kids.

After fixing her own plate, she started to grab a glass for her wine. She must have had a realistic look on her face, because her daddy asked, "So what's on your mind?" That was his way to start most of his conversations that ended in his asking about her job, followed by his backbreaking, 'I told you so' and calling her hard-headed.

Kirsten put the wine class away and grabbed a cocktail glass, so that before his next line of questions, she could deter him from talking about the real issues and instead, talk about her lifestyle in the city. By the time Kirsten had answered all the questions about who she was dating and every ex that he ever met of hers, she went off to bed. With a slight buzz, she kissed her mom's cheek and then, her dad's cheek and headed upstairs to her guest room.

The guest room was the only room in the house without a television, so Kirsten was left to herself with no source of entertainment and in the torment of her own thoughts. She felt guilty about lying to her parents about everything and even worse for not knowing how to tell that truth.

Kirsten's hopes to fall asleep seemed to be defaulting. She had spent an hour and a half just thinking of how she could love doing a job that she hated so much. Her goal was to make a plan that she could follow, but she could never seem to clear her head long enough to do so. Kirsten rolled out of the bed and headed for the kitchen to get the glass of wine she had replaced for a cocktail earlier when she was talking to her dad. She thought surely that would help her sleep.

She walked down the hall and noticed that the TV. was on in her parents' room, which meant her dad went to bed before her mom or that he hadn't gone to bed. She knew she ran a fair chance of running into him if she wasn't careful. Kirsten thought it was ridiculous to run from her family, but she still didn't feel strong enough to tell him that she thought she was failing as an adult. And, she definitely didn't want to hear the speech about how "It ain't easy out there, is it?"

Kirsten crept down the stairs, careful not to make too much noise and slipped into the kitchen. She poured her glass of cabernet and grabbed a mini cube of cheddar out of the fridge. As she headed back up the stairs, she sighed in relief that she didn't run into her dad, only to hit the landing and hear her mom say, "Who is that?"

"It's just me mom; I'm going back to bed. You want me to bring you something?"

"No, goodnight, don't forget to turn those lights out."

Kirsten's mom had a habit of talking in her sleep, so Kirsten just smiled said okay and moved on with her life. There were no lights on, and her mom probably didn't have her eyes open even to see.

She made it to her guest room and could only think of all the reasons why she should talk to her dad. She remembered the time he left the house, looking for her ex boyfriend, James. He'd stood her up for a date, and Kirsten held a straight face for two hours. She made up stories about him calling to say he was running late; she even went so far as to say his baseball game ended late. She did everything she could to keep her family from knowing that her feelings were hurt and that she was being stood up.

An hour later, James called to apologize; he had the most pathetic story ever, but he had flowers and candy for her every other day after that. He started taking her shopping and would obsessively ask if her dad had said anything about him. She later found out that her daddy dragged him out of the gym and scared him. She had never learned what was really said, but it must have scared some sense into him. So, even though Kirsten would try to handle things on her own, somehow her family would always help her.

Kirsten woke up Friday and got dressed to do her job. She had four appointments that day that were spread all the way out to 7:00 p.m. After her first two appointments, she went home to get her mom for lunch. It was almost becoming a tradition of there's that whenever Kirsten was home for work, the ladies would go out for lunch. Kirsten had been learning more and more about her mom that way, not that she wanted to know everything, it was just interesting and shocking, at the time, to hear that her prima ballerina of a mom had a little more juice than she had ever let on.

They finished their lunch at a new, little, Italian bistro, and Kirsten dropped her mom back off at home. She hated that her mom hadn't found anything else she loved to do since dancing. She hated even more that her mom had given up her dreams and had done so happily for her husband and her family. Now, she had to start all over. Kirsten, of all people, knew that starting over was the hardest thing for people to do. She wished so badly that she could help her mom find something she loved, but she couldn't even seem to help herself. At least one day, Kirsten thought she would be able give her parents whatever they wanted, and then, they wouldn't have to want for anything, especially not a career.

Kirsten finished a full day of work and was home by 7:15; she had planned on going out with her friends, but she didn't feel like it. Lately, going out had been the farthest thing from her mind, and her friends were too indecisive about what they wanted to do. So, Kirsten spent the next couple of hours watching action movies with her dad and her brother. Well, her brother and her dad were trying to see who snored louder.

After everyone else had fallen asleep, she tried to overcome her own anxiety. She still hadn't figured out the best time to tell her parents what was going on, and when the week started, she would have to face an evaluation in which she already knew what would be said. She was sure that her superiors would tell her "You're doing great; you'll be making big money soon." She knew they were only able to say that with a smile, because they sat on nice salaries and got bonuses on everything she did, so of course, the fact that she was struggling was null to them.

For the second day in a row, Kirsten spent the night in her room, wondering about her situation and the evaluation she was facing on Monday. What could she do? How could she make more money? How could she make her job work well for her? She thought so long and hard that waking up the next day seemed impossible. She woke up, realizing that she still hadn't talked to her parents, and leaving their plush bed to break up their smiles over morning coffee seemed even more impossible.

She finally got up and said good-bye to her family after deciding there was nothing to tell. Her daddy had worked so hard in his life that there was no reason he should have to worry about his adult daughter. If he could take care of himself and his family all that time, she could definitely work hard enough to take care of herself.

She usually went back to her parents' home after her last appointment, but this time, she couldn't wait to go. She had work to do on getting her lifestyle back and besides, this Saturday, she had plans, and it was one of the rare occasions they could all get together at the same time.

Kirsten had completed her first two appointments and had an hour to spare before the last. Since her small town wasn't large enough to waste time driving without going in circles, she took a trip to the only mini-mall in town. They had a small café that was nestled next to a bookstore. She ordered her favorite chocolaty drink and stared out of the window from a deep-seated comfy chair. She enjoyed knowing that she had made it the entire weekend without spilling her awful secret, but she knew that it meant she'd feel bad about it later. Now, she could wrap her mind around finding her missing serendipity!

Ms. Lawry arrived at her final appointment and learned that she had a meeting with her ex boyfriend's aunt, who apparently knew exactly who she was! James' family had always thought the highest of him and any woman who had ever been involved with him lucky to have the opportunity. Kirsten thought that James must have given his aunt her number; as to why, she wasn't sure. The meeting started off a little late, because all his aunt could talk about was how she heard Kirsten was still single and that James took great care of his children, even though their mother wasn't ready to be with him. She couldn't help but pick apart everything her potential client had to say. First of all, she was single, because she wouldn't settle for losers like her twenty something year old ex who still lived with his mom. Secondly, of course, he would take good care of his kids, because they were his possessions, so he would make sure they got the world handed to them on a silver platter. Finally, it wasn't the baby's mama who wasn't ready; it was James who would never be capable of loving someone as much as he loved himself. If he was so over her, why'd he lie down and have yet another child with her. Any woman who was good enough to have two of his big headed babies should definitely be good enough to be his wife, but that would destroy his baby boy syndrome.

Once his aunt had completed her list of reasons Kirsten should run back into the arms of her nephew, Kirsten was determined to have her say so before starting the meeting, so she could get back to her life and go out with her friends.

"Well, I am certainly happy he has found some balance in his life. I am sure his children are beautiful, and I know from experience that what is meant to be will be. So, if you would, tell me what you would like to do with your investments," Kirsten said with an innocent yet smug smile on her face. From her client's grin of embarrassment, Kirsten knew she had politely told her client to mind her own damn business and that her nephew was the only inferior being in the conversation.

She arrived home just in time, before she changed her mind about going out. She had spent the entire two hours thinking about how happy she'd be hanging out with her friends and how sad she'd be after looking at her bill. She rationalized her social outings, because they were the reason she was meeting more and more people. In her business, that was a bonus.

Kirsten didn't have time for a nap, and even if she did, she wouldn't have taken one. She spent most of her quiet time trying to make life easy again. She showered and dressed herself in a basic black shirt and dark denim jeans. By the time all of her friends had urged her to hurry up, she was grabbing her favorite biker jacket and walking out the door.

Once the group of women had finally gotten together, most of them seemed to be coasting through what was normally a cheerful and entertaining outing for them. Kirsten wasn't the only one trying to figure out her life, and it showed. Kirsten, Evelyn, Elle and Robin tried to hold stimulating conversations and flirt and have a good night out, but by midnight, the fun was over, and Kirsten was on her way home.

She was saddened that none of her friends seemed to be having life their way, because the energy of the group was completely different. They usually fed off of each other's vibrant personalities which, on that day, seemed to be impossible. Kirsten wondered how she could inspire her friends, but much like many other questions she had, she came up blank. On the other hand, she was rather relieved that they hadn't stayed out late, because then, she would have had a bigger struggle ahead of her in the morning.

Nine

"Therefore, you should not worry about tomorrow, for tomorrow will worry of itself," said the Pastor. As Kirsten gazed, focusing on his words, she also thought about all of the worrying she had been doing. She remembered a time when life seemed to be simple and joyful. Worrying had never been one of her habits before her carefree lifestyle allowed her more excitement than she could even imagine at the present time. Now, she had a hard time even getting out of bed in the morning.

She had been doing quite well at getting up and going to church. She loved church, only she hadn't been in a while. She heard of people who'd be compelled to go to church only when things were rough; Kirsten only wanted to go when things were good. She felt that it was better to go and share her smiles and hugs, than to bring people down with her serious face; besides, she was hardly in the mood to be pleasant during a negative and stressful time. She just decided to go to the 8:00 service so that she didn't have to run into many people, and she could be home before all the good movies came on.

She had gone to church and enjoyed it as much as she could, but as soon as it was over, she was on her way home. She passed on the standing around talking to people and went straight for her car, taking the message on humility with her. She was pleased to be learning and understanding the lessons life had to teach her and more pleased to know that she wasn't meant to be perfect. Kirsten drove home with the radio off, just driving; she didn't think about anything or about turning her phone ringer on, so she could hear if anyone called her, she just drove.

Once at home, Kirsten turned on her television to watch the marathon of chic flicks she knew would be on and climbed into bed. She had everything she needed and more. She started her movie day with sherbet and had spicy chips and apple juice for later. The only reason she had to get out of bed was to use the bathroom and answer the door after she ordered pizza, and even that was just a few steps away.

After her sherbet, she had watched enough of the first movie to know it was about some wife whose husband had gotten laid-off. He was so depressed that he never left the house. So, she was the breadwinner, on top of being mommy, daddy, and the maid for him and their three kids. She wasn't sure where the movie was going, but like most chic flicks, she was attached to the characters too much to turn.

She checked her cell phone to see that she had missed four phone calls, one was from her cousin and three from a familiar number in her hometown. Just as she began to think about whom the person could be, her phone rang again.

After saying hello, she heard Evan's voice say, "Hey, are you okay or are you just ignoring my calls?"

"I'm fine; my phone was just on silent from church. What's up?" asked Kirsten.

"Well, I wanted to have brunch with you, but it's almost 12:00 noon. Do you think you could be ready in half an hour?" asked Evan.

"Oh, well, I am already back in the city, but sorry, I would have gone with you otherwise," she replied. She was really thinking how happy she was to not be back home, because then, she would not have had time to make up an excuse not to go.

"I'm right outside; I'll come up and wait for you," Evan said.

"How did you know where I live?" asked Kirsten.

"I got your address from your baby brother," he replied.

Kirsten's heart jumped; she had not anticipated hearing that he was right outside. And, who was her brother to be giving out her address? "Why is he here?" she said aloud to herself. She was in such a bind. She had just said she would go, and now, she actually had to.

Kirsten let Evan into her place and began to ask a ton of questions. She wanted to know what in the world had possessed him to drive all the way to the city just for brunch. Their conversation seemed much more like an argument, until Evan said, "Look, I'm here, and you are going to brunch with me. Stop being such a pain and get dressed."

Kirsten cut her eyes at him and obediently stormed off towards her room. She managed to say, "Make yourself at home", before slamming her bedroom door. Kirsten was in her room, losing her mind. She walked back and forth from her closet to her dresser, looking for something to wear.

"I can't believe he is here! This is so ridiculous.... Who the hell does he think he is?" Kirsten went on and on about her surprise visit from her ex. She knew that it couldn't be good for her. She had put such a concentrated effort into staying out of a relationship with him. The fact was he had pulled her card. He knew exactly what to do to get to her, and the only thing that saved her so far were circumstances.

Kirsten jumped in the shower, quickly, to clear her head and speed up her process of getting ready. She felt as though she was dreaming, but she knew she wasn't. She just couldn't believe that he had come to see her. Maybe he had business here, and he just thought it would be convenient. She hoped he wasn't trying to get her back again. Maybe, that wouldn't be so bad; oh wait, she knew it would be bad. Kirsten remembered how he treated her. It was almost perfect. She had everything she wanted, and he could be so sweet. Not only that, he was one of those really strong men. Whenever she was with him, she felt safe and loved. Only, she could never grow as an individual when she was with him. Even when she tried to have her space, she couldn't; he became everything to her, and with him, there was no way for her to be an individual. Sometimes, it drove her crazy, but at other times, she felt like she needed him.

They were so cute together, and his proposal to her was the best. Evan had rented a boat and took a few friends and family members to the lake. He decorated the boat with flowers and petals; he even had Champaign bottles all over. When she asked, after they had gotten there, what was going on, he told her that the company he ordered it from had made a mistake, but since it was already paid for, he left it like that. Then, later that day, after everyone had eaten at the cookout, he took her hand and led her into the cabin off of the boat, where he gave her a beautiful, golden box. Inside, there was a cute, little, black dress with spaghetti straps and a diamond necklace to accompany it. Once she was dressed, he got down on his knee and said, "Kirsten, I have loved you since the day I saw you. I have always dreamed of having a wife as beautiful as you, one who would make my home a palace and make my life complete. Will you marry me?"

She burst out in tears, saying "I can't do that to myself." Kirsten cried the rest of the night, only clearing her face to say good bye to her friends and family, and if someone happened to ask why she had been crying, she just told them she had so much fun and that the day was so beautiful. She knew he meant exactly what he had said before, and as much as she loved him, they wouldn't work. He wanted a housewife to follow his dreams and to compliment his life, and all the months they had been together he had never grown to understand that her life was her own. She didn't want to complete anyone else's; she wanted to compliment it and vice versa.

Very few people had known about the proposal, and that is the way it would remain. They never spoke of it again after she stopped crying that night.

She would have still been in the room if Evan hadn't yelled to her "Kirsten, let's go; it's gonna take 20 minutes to get there." Kirsten finally got ready and walked into her living room where Evan was standing, ready to walk out the door.

Evan led the way toward the car. He was driving his favorite little corvette, which meant he would open the door, because he didn't think anyone else opened it with enough care. Kirsten hated getting in and out of the little bitty car. It was too much work, and as confused as she was about his presence, she managed to keep a straight face, but getting into the car made her face look like she was eating limes.

"Come on, baby, don't look like that. You know you're happy to see me," said Evan.

"Evan…get over yourself, I still am not too sure why you are even here," Kirsten replied.

"Get over myself, that's cute. I am over myself; I'm with you, right? You of all people should know that when I want something, I go after it, and I wanted to go to brunch with you, so here I am," Evan explained.

"No, Evan, why did you all of a sudden want to go to brunch with me? That's the question. You can't give an answer, because if you could, we wouldn't have spent the first fifteen minutes you were here arguing about why," said Kirsten.

"I thought we were friends; why are you being so mean?" said Evan.

"I'm not being mean. I just know nothing is that simple for you, but you try to make it seem like it's simple for everyone else. You think that you can just walk into people's lives, and as long as you take care of them, they're yours, and that's not okay."

"Kirsten, whoa…whoa…whoa! Sweetheart, I just wanted to see you; that's it. Obviously, you need somebody to take the pressure off you, because you just unloaded on me. That's not like you. Just relax, let me take you to brunch; if anything happens, it is what it is."

Kirsten took a deep breath and sat back in her seat. She knew there was no point in arguing, because he was right. She would just have to fight for her freedom if that's what it came down to. They took their 20 minute trip to the marina in silence. Kirsten didn't want to keep beating the brick wall she had run into with him, and Evan may have been offended by the way Kirsten talked to him.

Kirsten was so shocked to see that Evan had taken her to the newest restaurant in the city. She had talked about going to Dolce Villa on the marina with her friends. It was beautiful; they pulled around to the back of the restaurant and up the drive to the parking area. Kirsten sat there, as she waited for Evan to open her door. There were stairs cascading down towards the restaurant, leading to the most beautiful interior. It was amazing. Kirsten had forgotten about everything between her and Evan. She held his arm, slightly above his elbow, just as he had always liked, as if they had been together the whole time.

"Wow, the pictures of this place don't do it justice; this is amazing!" Said Kirsten

"This *is* nice, huh?" said Evan.

They walked in, and the suited man behind the bar rushed over and grabbed Evan's hand to give him a hug. He and Evan exchanged a few words until Evan introduced Justin, the owner, as his old friend. Justin escorted the two over to the table and said, "You guys enjoy; I'll send over my best server. You'll like it." Justin left Kirsten and Evan at his favorite table for them to enjoy his establishment.

Kirsten couldn't believe that someone Evan knew was the owner of the buzz around town. It seemed to be such a small world at that time, and for the moment, she felt as if she were on top of it. As she sat down, she said, "He is such a nice guy."

"Yeah, he is; we grew up together," said Evan.

"So, is that why you came here, because your friend invited you?" asked Kirsten.

"Yes, and that is why you shouldn't over react. We are thinking about going into business together. Hey, that's neither here nor there. Let's just enjoy!" said Evan.

"Okay, I can do that," she replied.

They ordered mimosas and were pointed toward the direction of the buffet. The spread of foods were fabulously laid out, and the duo had always been really good at engaging one another.

"I think you should try something new," said Evan.

"You always think I should try something new," said Kirsten.

"I'm serious; I'm gonna pick something out for you," said Evan.

"That's fine, as long as the same rules apply for you," said Kirsten.

Evan grabbed a saucer full of oysters for Kirsten, and Kirsten selected a variety of sushi for Evan. Neither of them was too fond of the other's choice, so they were sure to encourage sharing.

The entire time they spent at Dolce Villa was great. They laughed and did a lot of catching up. If anyone were to ask her, Kirsten would have to admit that she was having fun. The two completed their meal, still talking and laughing. Justin walked over to find out how they liked everything and suggested they take a walk down to the river. Before Kirsten had the opportunity to speak, Evan agreed, saying "Sure, we'll go down before we go to the car, but hey, man, your place is great. We definitely have to talk about some things. Can I come see you tomorrow?"

Tomorrow? Kirsten thought. She was under the impression that he would only be there for one day.

After the guys said their goodbyes, Evan grabbed Kirsten's hand to pull her up from the seat. They headed towards the back door, which was apparently the entryway to the outdoor seating area and the beginning of the trail up to the river.

Kirsten was unable to get over what a nice time they had. They walked up the river and back in about an hour, including their stop to sit in a small Gazebo that had iron statues in the middle of it. It was beautiful, as she felt at the moment.

Kirsten thought the entire trip back to the car about the kiss Evan had given her in the gazebo. She was entirely un-expecting of it but couldn't have stopped if she tried. This was the exact thing she talked about when she said she couldn't be her own person with him. He completely swept her away, when he grabbed the arch of her back to pull her to him. She fell right into his arms, allowing him to kiss her as intensely as he had when they were together.

Kirsten was in a daze; she had forgotten everything that weighed on her and gave Evan her full attention. She hadn't the slightest doubt about him at this point. She consented to going to the mall with him and even a play afterwards. She thought he was just going to pick up clothes to wear for the meeting he booked for tomorrow, but they walked around for quite awhile window shopping and talking and even taking advantage of the food court. They left the mall after passing every store and snacking at the smoothie place and then, headed towards the theater. Kirsten wasn't sure what was playing. She really didn't care; she was just glad to be having fun.

They sat and watched, as the mother and widow cried over her children's life choices. She knew that their father had worked hard to give them everything they needed, but still at adult ages, they acted as though they didn't have the good sense they were born with. Kirsten and Evan watched, as they made choice after choice and hurt their mother's heart. When the oldest found out that his wife was to have a baby, his yelling at her and his mom about how he didn't need any more responsibility made Kirsten curl up into to Evans arm. She stayed that way until the play was over and until Evan stood from his seat to pull her up.

After sitting through the three-hour play, the two ordered seafood dinners and took them back to Kirsten's place.

"Have a seat, Evan. Let me get you a plate," Kirsten insisted.

"Uh, Okay. I was gonna eat out of the carton, but plates work too," said Evan.

"So, since you have a meeting here tomorrow, why don't you just stay? I have plenty of space, and there is no reason for you to drive home, take a nap and come back in the morning."

"Okay, I appreciate that. Although, I probably wouldn't have driven home anyway," said Evan.

"Oh, so you were just gonna make yourself at home, huh?" asked Kirsten.

Evan laughed, saying "Uh, they do have things called hotels, Miss Lady."

"Oh, just eat. Stop laughing at me."

They ate their dinners, and she asked if he wanted to just sleep on the couch or on the sofa bed. Of course, he told her no trouble; he would just sleep on the couch, which was much more comfortable, in his opinion, than having the bars going across his back from a sofa bed.

After Kirsten brought out the blankets for him, he walked over to her to tell her what a great time he had, saying "Thank you so much for spending the day with me; I know you didn't have to."

Kirsten smiled, nodding her head, saying "Well, I had fun; it's been a while since I've hung out like that."

She hadn't remembered the last time she hung out with a guy that made her feel special and as if she didn't need to be in control all of the time. And, unfortunately, he was married, and she felt bad just knowing it. Though she was involved with him, her feelings were blocked by his situation, and even though he didn't care, it sure seemed to bother her. This was different; Evan was single, and she could remember, vividly, the way he made her feel. Even thinking of their history, she couldn't fight the feeling that she was having for him.

Once again, Evan pulled her into him and began to kiss her like he had earlier that day. This time, she let him hold her more willingly than the last. Thoughts were running through her mind about what she could say to stop the madness. She thought about saying, "No, I have to go to work in the morning," or "This just isn't right," but she couldn't. She wasn't going to deny herself someone that she had missed for so long.

Eventually, he picked her up to carry her into her bedroom, and Kirsten was pleased to know that everything she remembered about him and the way he made love to her was true. She wondered if he thought she was as perfect as she thought he was. Each move they made complemented the other's move, and when the height of their affection had been reached, Kirsten curled up next to him and laid her head on his chest.

Luckily for her, she had absolutely no energy left, because if she had, she would have been awake the entire night, thinking about the consequences of what she had just allowed to happen. Instead of her wallowing in her thoughts, she closed her eyes and slept peacefully on his chest, as if they had never separated.

Ten

Kirsten showered and dressed herself hurriedly, leaving her old fling there to sleep. She spent the thirty-minute drive to her office in somewhat of a daze. She was fully aware of the traffic around her, but she never bothered to turn the radio back on from her Sunday trip from church. Her thoughts were still tied to her activities of the night before, and not even the piss poor drivers could snap her out of it. In fact, she was probably driving like them.

"What the hell was I thinking?" she said aloud to herself. She knew that being with Evan that night was not going to help her situation and that she couldn't afford another emotional roller coaster.

She got out of her car after parking in the office garage and took her long walk up to the office. Being that it was the first day of her evaluation, she knew she'd have to face a million questions and make a ton of decisions based on what she wanted to do with her business. She had thought long and hard about leaving the company and still wasn't inclined to do so.

She took one step inside the door to see that they had acquired a new rookie. She was a little short, but she was blond and had light blue eyes. The two ladies spoke and even carried a few small conversations throughout the day, but after Kirsten had seen the entire staff of male managers fall over each other to cater to her, she decided she had had enough.

She wasn't jealous or angry; she just realized that she was in the wrong place. Her mom had always said, "People give you what they want you to have" and looking back at all of the opposition she had faced, she knew that she would never get ahead in the company. She called her friend, Stephani, out of the Ohio office, to tell her that she was done. It was almost like they spoke in code. After Stephani said hello, Kirsten turned on her cheery office voice saying, "Hey, I just called to let you know I was getting outta here today; I have some other things to do."

She sounded as though she was leaving for the day, but Stephani knew exactly what she meant; she was on the other end, saying "Wow, that's news! Have you found something else to do or what? You'll have to tell me what's going on."

Kirsten replied, "Sure, I'll call once I wrap some things up here, okay… thanks…bye." With that, their conversation was over, and Kirsten went down to talk with her boss.

She cut straight to the chase and asked, "If I leave, what happens to my clients?" He answered her question as best he could, which left Kirsten without an answer. She knew, regardless of what the answer was, she had to leave. She was slipping through the cracks in the company's infrastructure, and she didn't like it. She had slipped through enough cracks in her life to know that she could do better. She needed to go somewhere that she could grow, and her current position wasn't it.

"I am struggling with the fact that my job is to bring in business so that everyone has work to do. There aren't that many agents, and I was told that that would mean more leads and more support. I'm not getting it. It would be one thing if there wasn't enough to go around, but there is, and nothing is going around," said Kirsten.

"Kirsten, you have to understand that the people who survive in this business are those from wealthy backgrounds; they can sell one account and make more than you can make in months. If you can hang in there, we can keep you here," he said.

"I understand that quite well; that is exactly why I can't stay here. I am not from a wealthy background, and I don't believe that selling to my family and friends is what is going to make me successful. I can grow a business with no doubt, but to do it from scratch… I might as well be self employed."

"You are self employed, really."

"I'm not, because half of what I make goes to support an office that can't support me. There is no trade off," said Kirsten.

"I'm sorry, but I have to leave."

"But, Kirsten, we have a few details to work out first."

She ended her conversation with her boss and said, "Okay, well, I am on my way out of the office today, so we can work out the details later."

She walked out of his office and passed desks of people staring at her, as if they were trying really hard to stop but just couldn't turn away. Kirsten went around the office to the people she had a close relationship with; she saw Rick and Chanelle and a couple of others that she had gotten along well with. She let them know her plans to leave and after 4 hours of 'work' and an hour of exchanging contact information, she was on her way out. Sadly, she didn't have a job to go to, yet another of those things her dad told her never to do, but he had probably never worked a job where he didn't get paid to be there. So, leaving was much better than staying in her eyes.

Once out of the office, Kirsten called Stephani back, only to get her voicemail. She didn't bother to leave a message, because she knew they would talk about it later anyway. Besides, both of them hated checking voicemails that only said, call me later; it was such a waste of time.

Kirsten spent the next hour having lunch at her favorite deli across from her office building. She had taught herself to dine alone in college, and little did she know how much it would come in handy. She had convinced herself that the road to success didn't have to be lonely, but the more she sat in that deli, the more she found that it was. She knew that there was no one who could understand the path that she saw for herself.

Kirsten remembered that she had left a naked man in her home and wondered how he was managing. She called his phone and was sent straight to voicemail. Though she hated to, she left a message saying "Hey, just called to see how you were managing; call me when you get this." Now, she needed to know if he had left town already or if he would still be in her space when she got home. She took the scenic route home, just because. She now knew what it really meant to be flying by the seat of her pants, and she realized that she had been for months. Now, she had cut ties to the one thing she had been clinging to that drove her crazy…her job."

Kirsten came home to find Evan's car parked outside and went up to her apartment only to walk in, wondering where he was and what he would be doing. She still was unsure about how she felt about having him there; though they had fun, she knew it wouldn't work between them. They had too many differences in their life plan, and neither of them was willing to budge. She closed the door behind her and looked to the couch, where she saw almost everything that she'd looked at in the mall. She saw purses and suits and dresses on her couch.

That was one of the biggest surprises she had ever gotten. She didn't pick out anything that was cheap; there had to be thousands of dollars sitting there. In the midst of her surprise, came anger; she yelled for Evan and stormed through her apartment looking for him. He heard her call and ran out from her bathroom, asking "Baby, what's wrong?"

"Don't baby me, Evan! What the hell is this?" Kirsten asked sternly.

"What?! I thought you'd like it; that's everything you said you wanted," Evan defended.

"Bullshit, Evan! I asked you what you were here for, what you were trying to do and you had nothing to say. You can't just win me over with gifts. You know exactly what you are trying to do, and this time, it's not working…Evan, you know we can't be together," Kirsten argued.

"Look, I told you I wasn't try'in to win you over. What happened yesterday was great, but I had no intentions on making love to you last night. This is a gift; I would have given it to you whether I stayed the night here or not. I don't know what your problem is, but it's not me. I got you that stuff, because I closed a deal at my meeting today. I closed a deal, because Justin was impressed with you. I can't put you on the payroll, but I can buy you nice gifts," said Evan.

"That doesn't make sense to me; it just doesn't. I didn't even say that much to Justin," said Kirsten.

"You didn't have to say much; you wrote my business plan, remember! And, you looked damn good," said Evan.

"Like I said, I don't know what your plans are, but I can't afford the drama right now; I just can't. Believe it or not, you are drama!" said Kirsten.

The whole time, Evan stood there in his towel, trying to interject, but Kirsten kept talking. She was yelling, "I am just not ready to deal with this…" when Evan grabbed her and kissed her again. As tight as her muscles were, they slowly loosened up and allowed him control. She was experiencing the same feeling that she had the night before except there was no alcohol; it was broad daylight, and her anxiety from their argument was fresh. There had been so much tension between the two of them at that moment that they were out of control. This time, Kirsten wasn't thinking about how badly things could end; she was physically voiding all of the mental stress from that day. If this was why Evan came down here, he was definitely getting it, but Kirsten would have the last say in what he left with, and it wouldn't be her.

They crawled out of bed just in time for dinner, as Evan was reminded of the meals Kirsten had cooked for him. "What do you think about us cooking dinner together?" he asked. "Only if you aren't trying to make us something that we're not," replied Kirsten. "Okay, I saw a store off the highway on my way here; I'll go pick up some things." Evan threw on his clothes and went to the grocery store, leaving Kirsten to herself. She showered and put on a tank top and some yoga pants to lounge in and began to clean the mess that she'd helped create in her house.

Kirsten picked up her cell phone while she was cleaning and called her friend, Jada back. Before she was dying to tell her that she'd ran into their old friend, but now, she felt as though she had a confession to make. Growing up had made Kirsten realize that good friends make sure you don't do dumb things, and if you do manage to do something dumb, they are there to make sure you don't kick yourself too hard. She didn't know whether or not she was doing something dumb with Evan, but she knew she needed to talk about it.

Jada answered the phone and said her usual, "Hey, what's up?"

"You really are not gonna believe this," Kirsten said.

"Okay, is this a 15 minute conversation or a 50 minute conversation?" asked Jada.

"Well, I'll say 15, because Evan just left my house; I am sure he is on his way back," said Kirsten.

"You didn't. How the hell did he get to your house, two hours away from his? I mean, did this just happen? Okay, talk fast…"

"Well, I went home to handle those appointments, and of course, I stopped at the wine gallery. I didn't think he would be there, because he never is," Kirsten blurted.

"What do you mean you didn't think he'd be there; he owns it," asked Jada.

"I know, but he's hardly there. I thought we could be just friends. I handled it well; I left there without so much of an indication that anything was going to happen. I mean it's been years, Jada. Anyway, he kept calling me all Sunday morning, but my phone was silent. When I finally turned it back on, it was him, only I didn't recognize the number," Kirsten explained.

"Wow," Jada slid in.

"Just listen, I don't have much time. He was already in the city, and he wanted to go to brunch at his friend's place. Wish you lived here, I'd take you, but anyway, we ate, talked, went to the mall and then, to a play. We had so much fun, so we had dinner together. Then, we hooked up, a lot."

"TMI… Kirsten you know what he does to you…." said Jada.

"I'm not finished. I went to work and then, came home to a house full of gifts; we argued and did it again. Now, he is going to get dinner for us to cook together, but don't worry because we aren't trying to be in a relationship. Okay, now, you can go," said Kirsten.

"I can't believe you.... I just don't even know what to say. You've been here too many times, and you know how it ends. You are going to be heartbroken again, because you know you want him, and you know you don't think it will work." Jada said. She had seen all of Kirsten's relationships. They talked about everything, and she knew exactly what the conversations would be about. Once he was gone, it wouldn't be good.

"Okay, well, I don't have much to say, because I know, at this point, you aren't going to listen. So, I'll get off the phone. He'll come home with dinner; you'll eat and get back in bed with him. All I have to say is be careful; don't get yourself hurt...Have fun! Make sure you call me when he's gone, because you are gonna get it," Jada laughed towards the end.

"Thanks, bye," said Kirsten. Just like that, they were off the phone. Kirsten felt better that she had someone she could talk to, regardless as to how the situation turned out, but one thing Jada said made her rethink all of her actions. She kept thinking about having to call her when he left. She hadn't even thought about him leaving, so she didn't know how she'd feel. She still didn't know how she felt about him being there; she just knew she was having fun.

Kirsten piled all of her gifts in the corner of the couch; she wasn't ready to accept them yet, but she knew she didn't want her living room to look like crap. She could tell that Evan had tried to clean a little, because the plates and wine glasses were gone from the night before. She noticed that he'd even washed dishes. Kirsten realized that she really didn't have that much to do after all. She thought maybe she could vacuum, so she did.

As soon as she turned the vacuum off, she answered a knock at the door. Evan had finally come back with a grocery bag that looked full with more than dinner. She helped him to the counter and began to pull out the groceries. Kirsten pulled out some Italian bread, a package of pasta, salmon, shrimp, broccoli and some Alfredo sauce. She looked down into the other bag and saw strawberries, little cakes and some kind of fruit topping. They were preparing to fix one of her favorite meals.

They cooked and sipped wine, while they chatted about the deal Justin had just closed. They were going to build a little sister restaurant back in their hometown.

"So, Kirsten, are you sure you don't want to help me run the things back home? I am so sure your parents would like having you around," asked Evan.

"I don't think so, but thanks for the offer," said Kirsten.

Sure, her parents would love to have her, but they would also remember how complacent she had been when she was with Evan. None of her hobbies were ever important anymore. They would do most of the things that he suggested, and because he always had something planned to do, she kind of just got pulled along. Even though she had fun being a part of his life, he never considered becoming a part of hers.

Once they had finished cooking, they sat and ate together like old friends, watching movies and laughing at one another's jokes.

"This is great, Kirsten. I guess I should visit you more often," said Evan.

"I enjoyed you, maybe you should."

Before they knew it, Kirsten had asked a question that she didn't realize had entered her mind. "So why don't you have a girlfriend; I am sure some chic out there wants to be a housewife."

"I do," started Evan.

Kirsten sat there, dumbfounded, as the guy she had just shared the last couple of nights with told her that he had a girlfriend. Once again, she had unknowingly been made someone's sideline, and that someone seemed to have no remorse as to what he had done.

As Kirsten was drawing the conclusion that all men were assholes, she reminded herself that she was sitting right in front of one. She began to force the words out and focus on what he was saying. She realized she jumped to a conclusion; perhaps, he was going to say "I do, you are my girl, Kirsten." Only, that is not what Evan said.

"I have a fiancé," he finished.

"I don't fucking believe you; I never knew you to be such an asshole. You can go…leave!" said Kirsten.

"LEAVE NOW," she yelled.

Evan got up and grabbed his bag from her room; Kirsten didn't even allow him time to put some real pants on. They didn't say another word to each other. He knew she was pissed. She couldn't even form the words, but the look in her eyes said it all. She stood there, breathing heavily as she watched him walk out of her door in his shorts. As she thought to herself, "Oh, my god, how could I be so stupid? How could I trust him like that? Am I really that dumb?"

His foot hadn't even cleared the door before she slammed it on him, hitting his heel. She grabbed the door on rebound and slammed it again, after he tripped out of it. She turned the lock on the deadbolt and turned her own back towards the door, leaning against it. She had so many thoughts and emotions running through her head that she couldn't understand. The one thing she could say for sure was "I hate him." She slid down her door, until she sat with her arms over her knees holding her face.

For almost twenty minutes, she sat there thinking, no tears, no anger, just numb. It was 8:30 when she got up and slowly walked toward her room like a zombie. She looked at her bed and became infuriated; she snatched the comforter that was folded neatly at the foot of her bed before she could regain her composure. She stopped, took a deep breath, and began to take the sheets off of her bed, slowly; she was trying to convince herself that she wasn't angry and that she didn't feel hurt, but she knew she was.

Kirsten saw nothing between her and Evan and couldn't understand why he needed to lie to her or hide the truth. Lately, she seemed to be getting dragged into a lot. She had always been a sexier version of one of the guys; she wanted them to be honest and open with her. She had never been judgmental. She really didn't expect much from other people, so when she was found out that she was lied to or deceived, she had a hard time understanding why.

She finished making her bed over and climbed into it, just before her crocodile tear fell, and she continued to convince herself she was okay. Trying to suppress what she was feeling made her body so exhausted. Within the half an hour of her closing her eyes, she was asleep.

Her alarm clock went off at 5:45 a.m. She reached over to grab it and yanked the cord out of the wall. She thought how ridiculous it was for her to get up and go to a company that early, who had no respect for her time or efforts. The more she thought about their horrid systems, the more relieved she was not to be working there.

Kirsten closed her eyes and went back to sleep. By 10:00, her phone had been ringing uncontrollably. Her sister called; her mother called, because she didn't reach her at the office. Her immediate supervisor called to see why she wasn't at the daily morning meeting. Kirsten thought to herself that her supervisor must have been out of his mind; she had no obligation to go to there stupid meetings anymore. "He's crazy," she said aloud. She decided to call him back just to tell him again that she would no longer be a part of their sales team. Kirsten hung up from her voicemail and called her manager, saying "Hi, Jim, this is Kirsten; I just got your message."

"Oh, yeah! Well, I figured you weren't going to the meeting after my boss told me you quit, but we were wondering if you would take an assignment for us. Can you come in today?" said Jim.

Kirsten stopped her conversation, since he already knew what she was calling to tell him and stopped to think about going in for the other assignment. She thought that if she took the assignment, she could delay telling anyone, especially her parents, that she was unemployed. “Okay, I can do that,” she replied.

She forced herself from her bed and took her time getting ready for work. She moved as though she was in a hurry to get to the office, and honestly, she wasn’t.

Eleven

Kirsten still wasn't sure what had happened last night, but she was sure she was angry. She was missing all of the extremely nice guys that she thought weren't interesting enough and even the interesting one that had no life plan. It was the charismatic ones with the charm and good looks that were always too damn good to be true.

The way to work was just as numbing as the night before. Kirsten was in no hurry to go back to the place that she had wasted so much energy; she wasn't on a schedule, and she had no clue what she was walking into.

Arriving at the office just past lunch time, Kirsten cleared her personal items off of her old desk while she waited for Gary, the man who was responsible for her new assignment to return to his office. She took as much as she could out to her car before realizing how much she hated her environment. "Please hurry," she said to herself in regard to finding out why she had been asked to come. Just as she was ready to go back home and call it a day, she was called to Gary's office. He had a large office and his own personal secretary and a bunch of other perks for someone who never did any work. Kirsten tried to put her knowledge of his work ethic out of her mind, as she investigated their plans for her, but it was a little difficult.

Gary offered her a position in a temporary capacity, helping them to get caught up on compliance and community relations. The position sounded great to Kirsten; she would have limited flexibility, and it wasn't commission. She took the offer and spent the rest of the day hiding out, until she was actually given the clearance to do her tasks. Otherwise, she knew she would be bombarded with remedial requests of the office airheads that were more concerned with looking important than doing there own damn jobs.

Kirsten managed to get through most of the day, before she decided to go home an hour earlier than the other staff. She was spent. Most of her day was spent thinking about when she'd be able to look for another job, because she surely had no intentions on staying too long. She drove home, beating all of the rush hour traffic and stopping for dinner on the way. She picked up an apple pie to have something to indulge in. Kirsten heard her mom's voice in the back of her head, telling her that she wasn't eating a balanced meal and stopped for Chinese food to rid herself of feeling irresponsible.

"I can't believe this has happened to me," Kirsten said, as she opened her apartment door. She walked past the gifts from Evan, still in the chair, and tossed her apple pie in the oven and began snacking on her Chinese food, until her pie was done. That was it. She would spend the rest of her evening in silence. She had no desire to talk on the phone, and everything on television would have made her feel brain dead. She would sit, eat her pie, curse out her new least favorite person in the world and maybe even think of some poetic words that would help her feel better about her split decision to spend the last couple of days with an old flame. By midnight, she would have exhausted herself enough to fall asleep in peace.

Getting up in the morning had never been so difficult, but recently, it seemed more like work than anything else. This Wednesday morning seemed to be the roughest morning of them all. After her alarm sounded at 5:30, Kirsten realized it was set way too early for her new schedule. She had taken a new contract with her company to get away from a commission-based income. So, instead of her getting up to get as much done as she could in one day, she got up to punch a clock and do whatever she was asked to do, nothing more and nothing less. Knowing that the past few weeks getting ready had taken her longer than usual, she decided to get up at 6:30 instead of 7:00. Immediately after setting the alarm, she knew she wouldn't have the energy to get up in an hour; she hadn't had it in weeks. She stayed there, thinking about how she just wanted to stay wrapped in her warm, soft bed.

Kirsten thought about every reason she could as to why she should get up and drag the world by its ears, but her pillow top mattress and Egyptian cotton bedding kept her there. She thought of everyone who had ever commented on her ambition and energy and everything she had ever known about life being what you make of it, and the longer she thought, the angrier she had grown. Kirsten thought back a little more to everything she had done the past six months to go above and beyond, to learn everything she could learn. And, when she realized she was tired, she turned her head to bite her pillow, screaming aloud, “I can’t believe this, what did I do wrong?! What do you want from me? I have nothing else to give!” As she loosened the grip her teeth had on her pillow, she began to cry uncontrollably. In her anger, Kirsten was producing so much adrenalin that she threw the covers back and snatched herself out of bed, similar to a child with a temper tantrum. She walked, hastily, to her closet and snatched down one of her ready to wear suits. After throwing her dark grey suit on the bed, she headed off towards her bathroom, where she had thrown the previous day’s clothes on the floor.

After kicking the clothes, Kirsten realized how slovenly she was behaving and thought back to her headache, trying to ‘fung shui’ her life; she grabbed the clothes and tossed them into her basket. As she turned the water on and snatched off her pajamas, Kirsten caught herself mumbling, “This is so completely ridiculous; no one should have to wake up with a shitty disposition.” As she continued to mumble, “My life should not be like this,” she screamed “Ahhh-shhhiit!” Kirsten jumped, gritting her teeth; she had no choice but to calm down. At this point, she had just burned her skin to such a degree that it almost made her shed tears. Kirsten felt stupid; she jumped out of the shower, took a deep breath and continued her morning rituals more carefully.

Once fully dressed and after combing her long black hair, Kirsten stood there, just staring at her image in the mirror. For some reason, she knew she was missing something; she took out a pair of designer, silver earrings and put them on, which, for her, was rare. Kirsten hardly ever wore earrings; they seemed pointless to her, because her hair always hid them anyway. With no thoughts as to what she could be missing, Kirsten headed to her car to start on her way to the office.

"Just drive," Kirsten yelled, which usually was a good indicator that the rest of her day was going to suck as well. Road rage was definitely one of Kirsten's pitfalls; it meant that she was feeling impatient and restless. And, to her, anyone who stood in her way was against her. On a day like today, that included everybody, especially the people in her office that talked to her as if they were explaining something to a 3 year old, the phone calls with people asking if she were old enough to work there, and clients who would look at her and say, "Is there someone with a little more experience I can speak with?" None of that helped her in her attempt to rid herself of her tendencies to over prepare, and the past few days, she had been doing a lot of that.

Kirsten felt as if she had to know everything and to be accredited in her field before she could completely market herself, when really all she needed to know was the right person to ask. In her case, that was difficult; the people that were supposed to be there to help her were just as wet behind the ears as she was. That meant that, not only did she have to work twice as hard as everyone else to make what a veteran made, she also had to learn 10 times more than a veteran to get her career off the ground.

Before Kirsten knew it, she had pulled into the parking garage; luckily for her, she didn't remember anything but the way her drive started out. That meant the rest of her trip was smooth sailing. Unfortunately for Kirsten, her attention span is very limited. She could go from a-z and not pay any attention to the letters between the two. Being attentively challenged served for its own set of headaches.

Every time Kirsten entered the office, she felt as if she deposited a piece of her soul. Her smile only lasted long enough to greet all of the secretaries and assistants. By the time should could make it to her desk, she would run into at least two smug, middle aged men who could barely keep their heads out of the sky long enough to say hello, and if they could, they wanted to know how she liked her new position.

Kirsten sat in her cubicle, as she listened to the whispers and avoided the curious stares. Everyone was talking about her transition from sales to service. Most people in the support positions did all the work anyway, so you'd think reps would appreciate it. Really, any sensible rep would know that they can't service their clients without a service team. The problem was that one of the few sensible reps they had was moved to service. Kirsten didn't mind so much the work, just how people barked orders and fouled up procedures. Unfortunately, in her discomfort, she had nothing to do to keep her mind preoccupied. She had worked for this company for six months and enjoyed her previous position when she could come and go as she pleased. Now, she was stuck; all she could do was sit and wait for someone to ask for her help.

Kirsten spent her morning thinking that perhaps, her managers did her a service offering her a temporary position, and maybe, they were. She didn't have the energy to look for a new job immediately. Kirsten began to mumble to herself, "Who am I kidding, sure they were! I needed a job, because I definitely don't want to be in debt for the rest of my life, and the longer I go without a paycheck, the more debt piled up under her name." That didn't change the fact that going from an agent to a temporary associate was sort of painful, especially when someone throws it in your face. Everyone knew how much money an agent made or didn't make for that matter. "Well, I think, in the course of learning this business and being forced to be a hardass, some people don't realize when enough is enough," Kirsten told herself, and just in time for her manager's ironic request.

"Excuse me, Kirsten," her manager Jim asked.

"Would you take this list of all the agents to call and tell them about a change in a mandatory meeting?"

"Sure, no problem…"

For the most part, it went quite well; most of the agents were out doing what they where supposed to do or in the office getting caught up on 'down work' - at least they were courteous over the phone. However, one agent in particular, Greg Bruce, was the biggest jerk ever. Kirsten had met him before, but he didn't strike her as being a total asshole until that day. He had the audacity to point out my recent change in employment. First of all, only jerks answer the phone and just say, "Yes", like he had, Kirsten thought to herself.

I said, "Hi, Greg, this is Kirsten at the Main office."

"I don't know you, but what is it?"

"I am calling to make sure you are aware of the compliance meeting changes from the 4th of next month to the 11th. The time and locations are the same, only the date has been changed."

"Yeah, I got it; now, tell me about you."

"My name is Kirsten Lawry; we've met on several occasions, maybe you know me as a rookie agent."

"Oh, yeah! And, now, you are making the phone calls?"

"I am helping to get some things accomplished for the agency."

"So, you went from agent to clerical?"

"Something like that…"

"Well, bye," he said.

Kirsten couldn't believe, after replaying the conversation in her head, that he'd acted that way. By the time Kirsten hung up the phone, she went from being astonished to embarrassed, to just plain damn angry. "That was so rude, not as if it were any of his business." Kirsten had to think twice about what she was feeling, because she knew that she had a tendency to overreact. Kirsten thought about it again and reminded herself of how extremely tired she was of letting people say what they wanted to say or treat her however the hell they wanted, and then, she would get upset with herself for not reacting but being upset about it. "I am not a pushover; things do bother me, and for some reason, I am not as strong as I used to be to ignore everything," Kirsten said, as she shook her head.

As if her day couldn't get any worse, Ken Mathews, one of the sales managers, walked up. Apparently, he also thought that because she was no longer an agent, she was his personal secretary. Ken had the audacity to ask Kirsten to run his personal errands. For someone who only talks to people when he wants something, Kirsten felt he should never talk to her; she would do everything in her power to avoid helping him. “Kirsten, what are you doing today?” he asked. Kirsten listed of a bunch of things and turned back towards her laptop.

“Oh, I’m going have you do something for me,” said Ken.

Kirsten’s thoughts were quite clear, as she said to herself, “Oh, you are?” At least she thought she said that to herself, oh well if she didn’t.

“Yeah, the printers are not working, so I was going to send you to Kinkos for some copies,” Ken said smugly.

“Oh, well, you can order them online, and when they are ready…. you can pick them up.”

“Oh, can you order online now?”

“Uh huh.”

Needless to say, Kirsten had no intentions on going on any personal errands for anyone. The sad part is that Ken was determined to get her to go. Ken waited just as long as her supervisor, Gary came over and told him that he needed copies from Kinkos that he couldn’t get, because the machine was broken. Gary said, “Well, has it been pre-approved or just something you wanted people to have? Kirsten was so pleased that Gary told him to get them on his credit card; then, she smiled when she saw Gary hunch his shoulders, as if to say, “What the hell are you telling me for," which, for Kirsten, meant she could hold back the words 'kiss my ass' just a little bit longer.

Kirsten turned towards her computer to finish aimlessly reading through old emails when her phone rang. "Who has my new extension?" she thought to herself. As she grabbed the phone, she took a deep breath to prepare for whatever stress inducing person was on the other end. As Kirsten said hello, she realized it was an outside call; on the other end was what sounded to be an older man with a thick southern accent.

"Kirsten, this is Nathan Redman; we've never met, but I have heard a number of great things about you and am looking for some help in my agency."

"Oh, okay," said Kirsten. She had remembered his name from a conversation with a veteran agent, David Roberts; they had done a few appointments together, and before Kirsten had come back on contract in the department, he had asked if she wanted to stay in the business, because he knew a guy who would take care of her. Old agents always spoke fondly of what the business used to be like. They also talked about dirty agents, as if it were gossip for the locker room. Kirsten had been lucky enough to hear a lot of good things about this guy, as well.

"When is a good time for us to get together?" Nathan interrupted her thoughts. "I will only be here today, and then, I leave for Atlanta for a week to work on a case." he continued.

"What is your schedule like today?" asked Kirsten. She knew she couldn't wait over a week to see about her future.

"How about now?" he said.

"Sure!" Kirsten got directions to his office and went right over.

The entire ten-minute drive to meet with Nathan, Kirsten couldn't help but think of how miserable they attempted to make her at her old company. As much as she enjoyed doing her job, they made everything a struggle. She thought she had just been paying her dues, but she could see that she just didn't fit into their puzzle. She thought of the people who came behind her and were following in her footsteps. There were people that she trained with that were jumping ship nationwide; she thought that perhaps they weren't cut out for the job. Turns out, the company just couldn't handle new talent.

She had one friend, in particular, retracing her steps identically. She started super excited about everything that was promised her, and slowly but surely, as the promises defaulted, business declined, and anger triumphed, until the inevitable depression took over times that were once filled with the joy of being busy. Kirsten knew everything about Stephani and vice versa, which was quite ironic, considering that they had never seen each other. They started talking about training and the plans for their business and somehow, evolved to being weird alter egos of each other.

Kirsten hadn't talked to Stephani in days, which for two people who could predict each other's footsteps, felt like years. As a matter of fact, she didn't really want to talk to her; she felt she could do without anyone who could try and make her feel bad about her old married friend, from months ago. Especially since she didn't know what she was getting into. Kirsten hated being angry with her friends, but in her current position, she could care less. She had way too much on her plate and not having a friend to talk to may have added to it, but for her, getting her life together was priority one, and anyone who couldn't help her do that could kick rocks. In fact, the actual argument made Kirsten feel great, because for the first time in years, she had gotten the chance to yell at someone who cared enough to listen.

Kirsten stepped into Nathan's office and immediately noticed all of the awards. As he walked up to greet her, he said, "You must be Kirsten; it's a pleasure to finally meet you."

"Yes, hi," she replied.

"Well, Kirsten, I've heard so much about you; I feel as if I know you myself," said Nathan.

"I hope they were all good things," Kirsten joked.

"Sure they were; that's why you are here… I know enough about you to know that I like your work ethic, and if you want to stay in the business, I'd like to do everything I can to help you move your career along. So, if you are already fully licensed, tell me how far you have gotten in training," said Nathan.

"I am familiar with basic products, and I have a natural ability to make people talk. As far as training goes, there are probably many things I don't know. Maybe you could tell me what your training process is here?" Kirsten asked.

"We are different, in that we are a small company with independent agents, and usually, you don't see too many rookies as independent agents, not being first generation agents anyway. So, we aren't exactly set up for that. I am committed to making sure you know everything you need to know, so that's 17 years of experience, not to mention what you will learn from the rest of my team," said Nathan.

Kirsten new that the guy she was sitting in front of had credentials that she only dreamed of having, and once she heard independent, she knew she could do sale or work wherever she wanted. She struggled through the rest of the 45 minute conversation, as she could only think of the clients she would be able to sell to first and the amount of work she would have to do to get switched over. Kirsten left her meeting with a pile of contracts to look over and a headache from the self-inflicted rat race she was about to run. She knew, not only would she not have time for her friends, she would be cutting it close on any personal time that she had recently developed a need for. Kirsten had been disheartened about the way her career was going for the past couple of months, and after a few marathon events, when she learned she couldn't hide it any longer. Her life had become her going into the office around 5:00 a.m., and she didn't leave until 8:00 or 9:00 p.m. Sleep was a commodity for her; in her eyes, it was great to have, but she could go on without it for as long as she had to.

She had to get her career back on track, and doing compliance wasn't going to help her, neither was hanging on thinking about her relationships, or better said, old relationships. That meant she had to put James and Evan behind her and anyone else whom she could live without.

Part II

Control

"In the absence of self-control there is the presence of self-defeat."

Twelve

Walking back towards the office, Kirsten realized that something strange was happening to her. Her chest got tight and forehead started to sweat. She walked back to the office as fast as she could for more than one reason. One being, her breathing was so short that she felt she would pass out at any moment, and passing out in an empty parking garage after lunch meant a possibility that no one would find her until the support staff left at their usual 4:30 hour. The other reason was that she couldn't control how fast she walked; her body was so tightly wound that she moved at the same rate as her blood felt to be racing as it pumped blood through her body. Kirsten knew one thing, she had to calm down; she had to maintain her normal composure, and no matter what, she couldn't let anyone see how insecure she felt at that moment.

She coached herself back to the office the whole time, as she walked, telling herself, "You can make it, just a few more steps, and you can make it." As she simultaneously prayed, "God, I am too young for a heart attack," she continued to walk and with every step, could feel her pace slowing and her shoulders falling. Two men in suits walked passed her and looked at her as if she was wearing an alien costume. All she could see on their blurred faces was a distorted look of concern and confusion. Ironically, the one person in the at work whom Kirsten talked to was coming down the corridor. Kirsten recognized Chanelle from the office, and while looking at her face, her lips seemed to move in slow motion, but no words came out. Before she knew it, she felt as if she had been hit, flat across her face. Kirsten felt a burst of weak anger, as she asked herself, "Did that tramp just hit me? What the hell did I do to her?" As she felt her arm being pulled, she realized that she was on the ground and that the painful feeling she felt a moment ago was her face hitting the concrete floor. She had fainted, and Chanelle, the woman from the office was peeling her off the ground.

As Kirsten came to, she realized Chanelle was talking to her. She was saying, "I am so sorry I couldn't catch you; I asked if you were you okay, and you just fell before you could answer. Are you okay, what's wrong with you?" Kirsten knew that she was genuinely concerned for her.

Still, as she sat there on the floor, she realized she was still hot, and her breath was still short. She forced the exhausted words out of her mouth, and said, "I don't know, I feel sick." As she spoke, her mouth filled with hot liquid, and after realizing she was hopeless, she lost the fight she had been having with her body to get off of the ground. Kirsten looked at Chanelle and insisted, "Please, just let me sit here, just let me catch my breath."

Kirsten sat on the ground for what felt like an hour but was a mere two minutes. Chanelle stood next to her, asking a million questions. As sweet as she was, Kirsten was glad, at the time, that she didn't have the energy to talk, because she would have asked her to leave her the hell alone. All the while, her co-worker stood asking, "Can I get you some water? Do you need anything? Do you want me to call somebody?" All of which were very reasonable questions considering the circumstance, until she started trying to get all in Kirsten's business by asking, "Well, are you pregnant, because whatever the case may be, you probably need to see a doctor.

Kirsten immediately picked her dizzy head up and climbed to her feet, as she said, "Thank you, but I am fine! The only reason I would have to see a doctor is for the bones I probably broke in my face."

For some reason unknown to Kirsten, Chanelle insisted on giving her a hard time, as she put on her motherly face and said, "Well, it doesn't look like you broke anything in your face, because you can still move your smart mouth. If you won't let me call anyone, I will take you home myself. You cannot drive in this condition!"

Kirsten exclaimed back to her, "I don't have a condition; I said I was fine, and I don't appreciate having you yell at me about something so trivial. People fall all of the time."

Chanelle retorted back, "I don't have to know what made you fall down, but for the past seven months, I have seen you go from a bright, talented, young woman ready to take over the world to a barely functioning, shell of a person. The rest of these people might see you and think nothing of it, but you owe yourself more than a quick brush off the shoulder without a second thought. You still don't look well; you can't talk without slurring your words, and I know you don't have anyone to take care of you. Please stop being a hardass, and let someone help you for a change! I will drive you in your car; Rick can follow us in mine, but you can't stay here."

"I guess she told me…" Kirsten said to herself.

After a deep sigh, Kirsten agreed to the terms and began her way to the office to gather her things. With Chanelle at her side, she calmed herself down enough to think about what was going on. As the two walked, Kirsten thought to herself, she realized she couldn't afford to miss any time at work; she couldn't afford to stay out the next day, and she definitely couldn't afford to be falling out every time she couldn't clear her head.

In the office, Rick and Chanelle packed Kirsten's things in silence. Rick was too afraid to ask what was going on, and Chanelle didn't want to be the first link in the gossip chain, especially not while people walked by with careless ears. As the thoughts of being off work continued, Kirsten felt herself slowing down again. She sat at her desk, where Chanelle and Rick were helping her to grab her computer and her other bag, when out of the blue, Kirsten uttered the word "SHIT!!!" The word rolled off her tongue in slow motion. By the time Chanelle and Rick turned around, they saw tears rolling down her face and sweat beginning to bead off her head, as Kirsten slumped down in her chair holding her head back, as if she were trying to breathe.

Rick said, "Oh my God! Should we just call an ambulance?"

Chanelle said, "Honestly, I think we should, but she'll kill us."

"She can't kill us if she is dead!" snapped Rick. "I'm calling; I don't care what she has to say."

Rick picked up the phone and Kirsten whispered, "Don't, I just need to rest, just, please, just take me home." A gasping Kirsten and her two helpers snuck out the backdoor and headed down the hall toward the elevator. Kirsten was relieved that no one else had seen her in such a broken state of being.

Once in the car, Kirsten felt a little better; she realized thinking of work was triggering her discomfort. Knowing that she was too young for a heart attack, she started to think about the guy she'd met the day before, which she thought could be her husband. He was very attractive, had a great presentation and was very well spoken. Chanelle interrupted her thoughts of her knight in shining armor, "Look, I know you have been having a hard time here; do you think that is part of your problem?" "I don't I have a problem. I have been eating a lot of fast food, and I haven't been working out. It's probably wearing my body out. I am going to try and eat healthier and get some sleep."

"Girl, those burgers are not trying to kill you that fast; stop lying to yourself, at least not for my sake. I know how hard you have been working; I know how stressed you have been, and I know it isn't easy. I have been with this company for 10 years, and you need to realize that you are not the first and won't be the last. You are 23 and smart and ambitious; I know you know of other things you can do."

Kirsten chimes in with "but…"

"But nothing," assured Chanelle, "I said you are not the first, and you won't be the last. But, you are the only person I have ever seen go after something so hard. This job isn't for people as young as you; it's hard."

"I know, but that doesn't mean I can't do it!" Kirsten said.

"I didn't say you couldn't do it, but the odds are against you, sweetie. They can't help you. You need more support than what you have, and as a rookie, you can't expect to do it by yourself. You shouldn't have to."

"Go to another company that can train you," said Chanelle.

"I can teach myself; that's my point. Just because they can't, doesn't mean I can't," Kirsten said.

"You can, and I am sure you will, but not if you kill yourself first. You need to talk to someone; take this card," said Chanelle.

Her concerned friend handed her the card of Dr. S. Feylds. Kirsten looked at the card; she realized she had been given the name of a psychologist, not a recruiter or headhunter, a psychologist. Kirsten stuffed the card in her purse.

"I'll think about it. I don't need a shrink; I need a job," she said.

Silence fell on the two of them, as Kirsten fought back the tears. She knew everything Chanelle was saying was true. She couldn't do it by herself, and she definitely wasn't pleased to having been a crybaby that day. Kirsten knew it was time for her to leave. She just hoped it would work out. Chanelle broke her train of though once again to let her know they had made it to her building. Kirsten looked at her overprotective coworker and said, “thank you, I really appreciate it.”

“I know you do. Get some rest, and call me if you need anything, even if you just want to talk.” Said Chanelle

Kirsten smiled as if she were fighting tears once again, and as Rick and Chanelle headed back towards the office, Kirsten unlocked the door to her stark apartment home, only reminding her of all the bills she still needed to pay. She immediately threw her things down and called one of her closest friends, Robin. Robin was in med school and knew everything about everything; she practically could have been born a doctor.

To keep from telling Robin all her business, Kirsten left many details out. She also wanted to keep her from worrying about her. Robin and her other friends were already beginning to think she was acting funny, so Kirsten definitely didn’t want to give them more of a reason to trip. When she called, Robin was studying, as usual, so Kirsten knew she had to make it quick which, for her, was a good thing. She explained the symptoms and asked if it could be considered a mild heart attack. Robin said, “No, it sounds like anxiety, so that person is either seriously stressed or seriously disturbed or both. Why? Who are we talking about?”

Kirsten avoided the question by saying, “I just ask, no particular reason; it was just something I heard about.”

“Are you sure, or are you keeping something from me?” Robin retorts.”

"Noooo!" sighed Kirsten. "Everything is fine; just study, and we'll talk later. I just wanted to ask you that quick question."

"Okay, bye!" Robin grunted.

Kirsten hung the phone up and immediately began to look for the card to that shrink before she lost the nerve. Her plan was to call and leave a message, while she had the guts to do so. Unfortunately, for Dr. Feylds had an assistant that actually did her job, and the only message that was left was the one for Dr. Feylds that her 1:00 opening had been filled. If Kirsten had learned anything in sales, it was to set the appointment; everything else was a piece of cake.

Upon hanging up the phone, Kirsten went to her kitchen to find something to eat. She'd had enough fast food, and surely, she didn't have the patience to find someone to go out with, travel to a restaurant, wait to be seated and then, served. Her refrigerator was full of stuff that would probably send her to the hospital if she ate it. As she looked over the expired containers and day old take out, it was times like this that she was happy to live in such a busy area. She jumped in her car and went across the way to the super-center. On her way to the grocery section, she passed all of the appetizing snacks, the new CDs and a section of 'Sex in the City' collections that were half off. She walked past the treats and grabbed some chicken and a bag of frozen vegetables to make a quick stir-fry. She headed back towards the front to pay for her things and grabbed one of the DVD collections on her way.

Once at home, Kirsten managed to fix her food and found herself watching a marathon of Law & Order. She stayed awake until nearly 2:00 in the morning, before she fell asleep during one of the rerun episodes.

It seemed like only a few hours had passed when Kirsten woke up to head to her appointment with the shrink, only it was already 11:30. By the time Kirsten debated whether or not she would go, she only had forty-five minutes to get ready. She got up, forced herself to out of the door so that she could make it to her destination on time, and the fact that they held her credit card for a 'no show' penalty just in case she stood the guy up, made her decision quite clear. Her guess was that since her insurance wouldn't pay for the no show, he wanted to cover his time anyway.

On her way to see Dr. Feylds, Kirsten was very nervous. No one she had ever known had ever been to a therapist, at least not for stress, maybe a physical therapist. Unfortunately, she didn't even get to talk to the shrink, because her secretary set the appointment, not to mention Kirsten didn't bother to ask Chanelle about the referral. She already felt as if her work friend knew too much about her, though Kirsten wished she new a little bit about this doctor person. At this point, she knew she had to talk to someone who could help, because she was barely functioning.

As Kirsten parked her car and started toward suite 33 on the 17th floor of the building, she couldn't help but to think how she'd love to get her own office in a building at least half as beautiful as this one. The floors had a glow that fell off the glass exterior onto beautiful, neutral colored, marble floors with sterling planters scattered throughout the building and the most pleasant receptionist she had ever encountered. The receptionist said to her,

"Hello, do you know where you're going or would you like for me to show you in the right direction?"

Kirsten took her eyes off of the décor long enough to say, "Will you point me towards the elevators, please?" After getting her answer, she realized she needed further directions to her destination. She just couldn't bare anyone knowing she needed to see a shrink, not even the sweet, little welcome girl, who was probably much younger than she was and more than likely, had no idea what she was there for.

On her way up the elevator, Kirsten thought to herself how much she could be doing to make her life better. Instead she was wasting an hour, not to mention travel time, talking to some doctor, who probably can't help her. As Kirsten got closer, she realized the tension was building, and the longer she thought about the waste of time she was about to embark on, the more frustrated she became. She could have been putting her files together, contacting her clients, sleeping, anything other than talking to a shrink. After turning red in the face, she had finally reached her destination and just in time, too, or the handsome secretary would have seen the beginning phases of her most dangerous enemy, her anxiety.

As soon as Kirsten opened the door, she found herself staring at a 30 something, GQ cutout with a perfect, dark skin tone. His suit was a dark blue with almond colored stripe. He wore the suit jacket opened so that his light blue shirt and his brown and blue multi-shade striped tie both hung perfectly on what looked to be a well chiseled body. As he looked at her and said, "Hello," she realized he was standing over a middle-aged woman with blonde hair, who smiled and said, "Can I help you?"

"Yes, I have a meeting with Dr. Feylds," Kirsten replied. As the receptionist buzzed Dr. Feylds, Kirsten was suddenly confused as to whether or not she was disappointed that Mr. GQ wasn't her doctor or that she didn't have time to spark a conversation with him.

"Your 1:00 is here" the secretary said.

"Send her in, please," replied the woman.

Kirsten walked in the direction that was shown to her, until she reached the halfway opened office door.

"Hello," said Kirsten.

"Welcome, Kirsten, right?" said the woman.

"Uh huh," said Kirsten with a nod.

"Hi, Samantha Feylds, to what do I owe the pleasure of meeting you?"

"Well, you were referred to me by a friend, because I had a small anxiety attack," said Kirsten.

"A small attack… tell me a bout it," questioned Dr. Feylds.

"Well, I kinda fainted on my way into the office. I was sweating, and I got short of breath. Once I made it into my office, the shortness of breath thing and the heat came back. Two of my coworkers helped me to pack up, and the one who drove me home felt I was working too hard," said Kirsten.

"What do you mean by working too hard?" asked Dr. Feylds.

"I do a lot of work, and it's yet to be profitable for me. I don't know; sometimes, I agree that I am working and getting nowhere, and frankly, I can't afford to waste any more time on something that is going nowhere," replied Kirsten.

"Well, Kirsten, I have to tell you that our mutual friend did call to see if I could help you. Don't worry; everything that we will speak about is confidential. You shouldn't let your work life have such an affect on you. You seem like such a talented, well spoken woman, and in my line of work, I talk to a lot of people with work problems and life issues. You shouldn't blame yourself for what is happening to you; it's normal. You can either hold on to what you have already and run the other way, or you can try to make it work, but perhaps, we can get to the bottom of that," said Dr. Feylds.

"Well," Kirsten began to talk. After a brief moment of silence, she said, "My mind is blank."

Dr. Feylds interjects and says, "That is just fine. The reason we are meeting is to help you overcome the issues you are having, and I believe that that is a great place to start."

"I don't know where to start," replies Kirsten.

"Start by telling me whether you want to try something new or just keep trying in your existing position."

"I guess I am still sitting on the fence," says Kirsten.

"Please, tell me what you mean, Kirsten," the Dr. responded.

After a short pause, Kirsten starts, "I guess I haven't chosen a side, but I am leaning towards holding on to everything I have. I quit my job, but interestingly enough, they asked me to come in under a contracted staff role."

"Were you happy about that decision?" Dr. Feylds asked.

"Worked for me at the time! I am, or was, a Financial Advisor, but the commissions started to kill me. I wasn't really making enough money, so it felt good to have someone offer me something with a guarantee instead of stressing about not getting paid at all. The way they set it up, I was able to sell independently and work an hourly schedule," said Kirsten.

"Tell me about your experience with sales and commissions; I have a few clients who are also annoyed with a similar situation, especially with the economy the way it is," Dr. Feylds urged.

"I have only been at the company for seven months, and I have been 100% commission for about 4 months. So, for 4 months, I have the distinctive experience of pulling my hair out, screaming into pillows, drinking excessive portions of alcohol, crying, biting heads off and sleeping at unusual times of the day. All of which you would probably diagnose as something terrible that would cause any member of the medical profession to suggest some drug that could cause heart problems, diarrhea, and cottonmouth or could possibly result in death," answered Kirsten.

"Hahahaha"... they both laughed.

"Now, we don't know that, but it's nice to see what you think of my profession," she said.

"Hahaha"… they both laughed, again.

"Let's continue. How did the people close to you respond to your behavior?" said Dr. Feylds.

"Fortunately for me, none of my friends or family members knew how extreme of a situation I had created. I have a really bad habit of smiling for everyone and trying my damnedest not to cry or complain," said Kirsten.

"So, you didn't talk to anyone about what you were experiencing?" asked the doctor.

"I didn't say that; I didn't cry or complain. I just said I tried hard not to. I would talk about the facts, but at the end of the conversation, I was smiling and hearing myself say things like, 'but I can do it, and they won't get the best of me.' I think the only way I made it as long as I did in the business I was in was that I had everybody around me convinced that I could do anything I put my mind to; I probably can, it is just a little difficult without a certain level of security," Kirsten said

"What do you mean by security, like self-esteem or like protection?" said Dr. Feylds.

"Security, I guess, is something I learned about from that college degree that I am not using quite yet. Do you know anything about Maslow and his theories?" said Kirsten.

"Sure, so you are saying your needs weren't being met? Do you mean personally of professionally?" she asked.

"I'd have to say both. If my career hadn't flopped, I would have been so wrapped up in it that I would not have paid any attention to my personal life," said Kirsten.

"Let's start with the professional then," suggested the doctor.

Kirsten took a deep breath in order to brace herself; she had never openly admitted to anyone that she had failed at anything, at least not with sincerity. Once she convinced herself to talk, she said "Well, I joined a large company, because I thought there would be a lot of support. Also, since I was the only new employee at my company, I expected to have a lot of attention and resources at my disposal. Wrong! The attention and training I received was, 80% of the time, from people who sucked royally at what I did and were granted management positions to beat the heat. Another 10% came from support staff who would have done anything to help me but just weren't in the position to, and the other 10% came from wholesalers and internal support, who I wish I had known to ask for help from in the beginning."

"What about people close to you? Did they support your career?" Dr. Feylds asked.

"They did as much as they could, anyway. I don't come from a wealthy background, but people bought what they needed and could afford. Unfortunately, with all of the sales I made, it still wasn't maintaining my lifestyle. That was one of the reasons I decided to leave. I would say that there was one person that knew everything I was going through," said Kirsten.

"Care to tell me about this person?" asked Dr. Feylds.

Kirsten sighed in hesitation before she spoke. "I can; I met her before I became a disgruntled employee. I received an email from a new employee, Stephani Milton.

It was probably my third month in the business and her first. If I remember correctly, she sent an email to me, hoping we could talk. I was almost jealous, because even though I had a college degree and thought I had a good vocabulary, her email was pristine; the grammar flowed perfectly, and all the punctuations, which I had forgotten how to use, seemed to all be in the right place. So, I was impressed with her writing style, but her content was like, so arrogant, and the only reason I replied was because she dropped the name of this guy, Joe that I worked with. I figured if I thought he was a great guy, and he thought enough of me to introduce us, then I could at least respond to her email. After my reply and our first telephone conversation, I had confirmed that I didn't like this individual and planned not to talk with her again, and little did I know how false my confirmation would be. For some reason, I ended up talking to everyday, if not several times a day, so we actually turned out be good friends."

Dr. Feylds then asked, "Do you still talk to her?"

"I do… but not as much as I used too. We kinda got into a big argument and stopped talking for like, two weeks, and now, we just talk whenever, more out of courtesy," said Kirsten.

"What kind of argument?" Dr. Feylds asked.

"I think we might want to save that one for another meeting," said Kirsten.

Kirsten thought of whatever she could to end that conversation. In her mind she had no intentions on going back anyway.

"So, it was a bad argument?" the doctor asked.

Kirsten looked at her as if she really didn't see why she was taking the conversation in this direction and said, "It was just about a guy that she disapproved of, and she had no problem letting me know that she didn't care for our relationship. Personally, I was working like 90 hours a week, and I had a short fuse, so I called her a judgmental asshole and hung up on her."

"You want to tell me a little bit more about the guy?" asked Dr. Feylds.

Kirsten shook her head and said, "I'd rather not, but we could go back to talking about work."

"I sense that you are getting a little uncomfortable. Why is that?" she prodded.

"Look. You are asking me about, stuff that I don't talk to myself about and you want me to just give an answer. I don't doubt that you are good at what you do, but where I come from, people don't talk to shrinks," Kirsten said.

Kirsten began to get angry, and Dr Feylds looked as if she didn't expect her change of character. Dr. Feylds took a regretful sigh and comforted Kirsten by saying, "It's okay; we don't have to talk about it now. I understand how people can feel uneasy about conversations like this. We have a little more time, and we can talk about whatever you want to talk about." At this point, Kirsten felt vulnerable and embarrassed; she realized she had just snapped for no reason, and whatever emotions this conversation had brought up were about to come rolling down her face. Kirsten quickly sucked it up and said, "No, thank you, Dr. Feylds; I have to go."

She left the room so fast that all Dr. Feylds had a chance to say was, “please call me, Samantha.”

Thirteen

"Just call me, Samantha, I can't believe her, the audacity," Kirsten was upset and for no good reason. As she walked to her car, she realized she had to pay for a whole hour regardless as to how short she cut her time. Now, she was upset that she was wasting money. "I don't think she did a damn thing to help me." Kirsten realized the people in the cars next to her were looking at her as if she were crazy, so she immediately stopped talking to herself out loud. She thought this could be the reason that no one she had ever known went to see a therapist.

After Kirsten's usual long ride home, she decided to fix herself a steaming hot cup of chamomile and lavender tea. Somehow, she had learned that it helped her relax after snapping at people on the highway and just a generally crappy day. If the tea wasn't enough to ease her mind, and if by the time she had had just a little too much in a day, she could drink a nice glass of Cabernet or a Shiraz and put herself to sleep.

As she sipped her tea, she sat on her couch, trying figure out what to do with the rest of her day. It was only

3:00; she had a whole day to pass. Clearly, she could have found something more productive to do, but her brain felt so overwhelmed. She settled on her recently acquired purchase of "Sex and thc City" the entire series; she had watched the show for so long and for the most part, never saw any of the shows in order until the end of its time on television. She bought the series, because she'd heard that the movie was coming. Kirsten and her friends had decided to see the movie together, so she needed to catch up in order to not break the no question code. She popped in the dvd and started to watch episode one of season one.

Shortly after she started the series, she had fallen asleep, so by 6:30, she had been taking at least a three-hour nap. Kirsten was so tired that she hadn't even seen the entire first episode, nor did she notice that she missed seven phone calls. As usual, when Kirsten missed that many calls, it was a combination of solicitors, her mom, and the occasional guy friend. Kirsten managed the calls in order of priority; she ignored solicitations for the time being and then, called the guy friends to tell them she missed their call, but she'd have to call them another time. She didn't want them to think she was blowing them off. Josh had been one of them. He first answered the phone, saying "Hey gorgeous."

Kirsten was somewhat thrown off by his choice of greeting and replied, "Uh, hello… look I was just returning your call; I am in a crunch for time, but I didn't want you to think I had ignored your call," she said.

"Nah, I was just calling to say hi," said Josh. Okay, you said it, Kirsten thought to herself.

"Okay, well, you take care. I will speak with you some other time then." After that, Kirsten ignored all other attempts he made to stay on the phone with her.

Finally, she called her mom, because at a time like this, her mom tended to have some weird sixth sense. Kirsten would have to deter her from thinking anything negative, that past summer, when Kirsten's mom tried to put out an APB on her during her trip to Detroit this past summer.

Kirsten packed her weekend bag so that she could start her trip to go see a Beyonce concert. The trip to Detroit was about a five-hour drive, but it was worth every minute. Unfortunately, Kirsten was extremely tired; she had only taken a one-hour nap after being awake all night for her casino trip the night before. Kirsten had left a get-together with her friends and realized that she didn't, in the slightest way, want to go home, so she set off to Chicago which was two and a half hours away. So, even with it being 1:00 a.m., she drove to the casino.

It wasn't that she was dying to gamble or to have an adventure; it was that she didn't know where to go next. Home no longer felt the same to her; it no longer had a sense of security, because she wasn't sure how long she'd be able to afford it. She was lost. She was exhausted of any inspiration or common sense; all she had left in her mind was confusion, so she followed the only idea she'd had.

Once she arrived, she realized that even at this early hour, the place was full of people, who had nothing better to do or who had developed a habit that was more than likely too much for them to handle. She walked past many people, staring for whatever reason; perhaps, it was because she looked too young to be there or maybe, because she was alone. Whatever the reason, she didn't care. Kirsten was more concerned with why she had already wasted 2 hours of driving time on such an impulsive decision. Kirsten walked onto the boat; she realized she had nothing to do either. The same boat that had called out to her now left her pathless. She had no idea which direction to go. Her usual decision-making was null, and she was alone with no one else to help her.

Kirsten walked down the long corridor to what looked like a food court. She figured she would stall time, but she had no appetite and no desire to sit in front of a plate of food with a pathetic look on her face. She took one more glance over the place and noticed a ladies room. With a sigh of relief, she headed towards it, thinking she could go in and get her thoughts together, when two guys looked at her and smiled, saying "Hey, where your people at?"

They were completely miss-matched; one wore a law school T-shirt with perfectly fitting jeans, and the other wore an oversized t-shirt and jean ensemble with a baseball cap, not to mention his big gaudy neck chain.

Kirsten knew exactly what they meant, but she played innocent, saying "What people?"

"You know, your girls or your man or whoever you here with," the smart guy said.

Kirsten, being in a reckless mood, decided against her usual safe mode by making up company to give the impression that she had back up. She gave a flirty smile and said, "I guess I'm my people today."

"Naw, you ain't," said the baggy guy.

"Uh, yeah, I am, why?" she said.

"It's just that you really don't look old enough to be here, and if you are, you are too pretty to be alone?" the smart guy spoke shyly.

Kirsten studied them both, quickly, before she said anything else. Not sensing any harm, she said, "Well, when I make up my mind to do something, I do it, with company or not. I wanted to see what the boat was all about."

"You never been to the boat?" said baggy.

"No, I never been to the boat. Why you wanna show me how to gamble?" she said, somewhat mocking them.

The three headed off towards the 'game room' with Kirsten leading the way. They could have been behind her, because they were checking her out or just because they didn't know where they were going either, but Kirsten had decided they weren't going to make the cut. Soon after they got into the 'game room,' she said, "Well, I'll see you guys around" and headed off to find something to do. They hadn't played any games together or even exchanged names, and that was just it. She had no desire to have two pointless tag-a-longs. She felt that she couldn't even carry her own weight, let alone two random guys.

As lost as she looked, some really old guy must have seen her, because he said "Hey, lil' lady, what are you doing in a place like this?"

Kirsten wondered why people ask such dumbass questions like that and said, "I'm just checking it out; maybe I'll learn something."

He smiled and said, "Maybe I can teach you something, come here. You ever played craps?" Kirsten walked over, shaking her head no, as he pulled out a stack of money, saying to the table, "Hey, guys, let's show the lady how to play."

Kirsten sat and watched and took a couple of guesses for about half an hour, when she realized she had no purpose there. She was in the business of making money not throwing it away; she was sending herself the wrong message, whether it was her money or someone else's. She thanked the players and chatted for a moment with the men who had tried to teach her to play before she stepped off of the table. Thinking she must have lost her mind, she abruptly said, "I'm going home." She walked past the two guys she first met walking in and smiled at them, saying "See ya!"

"Bye, cutie," the baggy dude said, while his friend said, "take care," and she was off.

She sat in her car, trying to put together how remedial she had to be to go on a trip like that, knowing she had to drive 5 hours and had a party weekend still to come. In her state of tiredness, she shed a few tears about how miserable was feeling, being so tired yet so restless. Kirsten took a deep breath and started her 2 hour plus trip home. Her daddy had always disliked her driving habits, but the one he hated most was her driving in the dark. Not only was it dark, it was nearly 2:00 in the morning; she was alone, and she had to stop for gas. But, that was the least of her worries. She was sleepy.

Kirsten cranked up her radio, listening to whatever station that didn't have a commercial and tried to sing and jam along with the record. It worked for about an hour until she started to feel herself fall asleep. Kirsten stopped at a rest area halfway through her trip. She had passed her 'I don't care' phase and was now scared; the rest area she had driven to was dark and empty with the exception of a few truckers. Not liking the situation, she drove another 15 minutes, until a large deer jumped out in front of her with glowing eyes. Kirsten jumped, as her eyes popped open in shock, and her heartbeat was as fast as if she had overdosed on cough syrup. She had fallen asleep, and that deer dream probably saved her life. Kirsten took a deep breath and pushed herself to the next exit. She pulled into the gas station, set her alarm for ten minutes and took a nap. Kirsten had planned to inch herself home and stop every fifteen to twenty minutes, which was about how long it took to reach the next stop, so instead of her last leg being an 1 and ½ , it was 3. She finally made it. It took some swerving, but she made it, praying the whole last twenty minutes, "Dear God, I promise if you let me get home, I'll never do anything like this again; I didn't even have fun," and uttering please and thank you, until she was in her bed taking a nap.

Kirsten's nap was cut short by Camron's phone call. He would often call to see if she had done an early day at work. She quickly ended that conversation by telling him she had just gotten home about an hour ago, and she was trying to nap. He usually got angry when she was out, and it wasn't with him. The last time, he threw such a fit that

Kirsten had to remind him that he had a wife. Then, her sister, Aubrey called to say how excited she was to complete a project at work. It was the first day she had gotten up before Kirsten, and that was because she didn't have to work late the day before. Kirsten realized her nap was over and got up to pack while talking to her sister.

"So, now that I know why you are up so early, please tell me why you called me so early," Kirsten said.

"You are always up early. What makes today any different? What, you didn't have to get up early today?" Aubrey shot back.

Kirsten usually spent Saturday mornings working or doing some kind of community service project, so the fact that she was still asleep was shocking to her sister. Aubrey knew Kirsten was going to Chicago, but she didn't think she was serious; she didn't know that she had planned on staying nor did she know the concert was in Detroit. Not that she was hiding anything, Kirsten just didn't feel the need to tell her everything; it was just one of those 'you didn't ask…' moments. "No, I didn't volunteer today, but I did just get home a little while ago, well before my nap," Kirsten answered.

"In from where? You are not in college anymore; real adults don't party all night," Aubrey assumed.

"I didn't say anything about a party; I just decided to go to the boat after hanging with my friends," Kirsten answered.

"What?! What the hell is wrong with you? Since when do you go to the boat in the middle of the night? Who went with you?" Aubrey asked, as if she would be mad at that person, too.

"Uh, remember who you are talking to. First of all, you ask too many questions at once. I went by myself, because I wanted to go. Now, I'm back; it's no big deal dude, relax. Anyway, I have to pack; I'll talk later," Kirsten said in her 'get over it tone'.

"Bye to you, too," Aubrey said, after realizing her little sister was already gone.

Kirsten couldn't believe she called this damn early in the morning trying to lecture. She knew she meant well but would rather not have to listen to it. She walked into the living room of her apartment to turn on her radio. Kirsten sang along with her stereo and prepared for her trip to Detroit.

Kirsten's phone rang once again, interrupting her preparations for her trip to Detroit. She had gotten into the habit of answering most of the local numbers, even when she didn't recognize them. She didn't want to take the chance on missing a call from one of her clients or not even potential clients for that matter. Her mind was made; she had made it up long ago that she would be the epitome of a businesswoman, and this time, she was going to put her all into it. Ironically, on the other end of the phone was an associate of hers, Shelly; she wanted to borrow a book, and Kirsten told her she would drop it off. Kirsten got her clothes together and threw them in the car. She noticed that the car she'd always kept so tidy now looked as if animals lived in it. There were half full, fast food cups in the cup holders; her carpets had tiny rocks from outside on them, and her seats were covered in random brochures, church programs and junk mail. As disgusted as she was with the interior of her car, she persisted in throwing her bag on the back seat.

As much as Kirsten hated pumping gas, she was off to the gas station to fill up for her trip; while she was there, she could at least dump the trash out of her car. She waited for her little Volvo to fill up while she piled the mixture of messes on her back seat so that it didn't look so bad from her rear view mirror.

Once at Shelly's, she'd left the book on her front porch and was on her way to the music mecca to hang out with her friends and get away from her own lifestyle for a few days. Surprisingly, her mini-nap had given her enough energy; she started out on her trip, listening to the local radio station. On Fridays, they played non-stop music, and it was mostly a mix of old and new. The first hour of her trip went by fast; the rest of her trip probably would have if she hadn't run into traffic. It never failed. When she was on a time schedule, she would be sure to run into traffic, and by her second hour of driving, she had slowed to 50 mph.

She and Jada had been planning this trip for a few weeks. Jada warned her to leave extremely early. Kirsten agreed that she would, but she hadn't, at the time, planned to go out gambling the morning of. She also hadn't told Jada that she did. She got to Detroit just in time to get ready quickly and grab a sandwich. Kirsten stopped at the first place she saw, grabbed some food and finished the last fifteen minutes of her trip to her friends.

She walked up the stairs to her friend's apartment. When Jada came to the door, she immediately said, "Didn't I tell you to leave early?"

Kirsten laughed and said, "Whatever, you're just happy to see me." She hugged her friend and went straight to the guest bathroom to get ready. "I'm going to need you to hurry up..." Jada said. Kirsten ignored Jada's comments like she knew she was just ready to go. Neither of them were fans of waiting on other people. That's one of the reasons why they made such great friends. They hardly ever had to wait for the other, and if they did, it was okay. They were both very considerate and enjoyed most of the same things. Most importantly, they understood each other.

After Kirsten got dressed, she went through the apartment, looking for Jada. Jada was on the phone with another friend who was supposed to meet them at the apartment but decided that she didn't feel like stopping, so they should just hook up at the concert. Jada was pissed. At this point, waiting for her at the house was the plan they'd made weeks ago. Now, she would have to get there and try to find her through the hundreds of other people at the concert, which would probably make them later than if they had just waited for her. Kirsten teased Jada, because she knew how much she hated to wait. She even made the joke when she got there; she wouldn't be the one to make them late.

On their way to the concert, they popped in a few CD's to get in the mood for the concert and to pay less attention to the mounting traffic they had run into. They took a twenty-minute drive, only to wait another twenty to find parking.

They saw more people they went to college with in the concert parking lot than they ever saw in a class. Jada and Kirsten took the long walk past the T-shirt sellers, the different groups of people standing around and the red carpet, leading from the pre-show that they had missed but didn't know anything about. They even found themselves waving and greeting old college friends the whole way to their seats. They partied like they had front row seats for the entire concert. By the time it was over, they found themselves hoarse and excited about the night's events. On the way home, Jada mentioned that a bunch of her friends were planning to go to a nightclub for an after party. Only Jada hadn't realized that Kirsten had fallen asleep minutes ago; the only thing Kirsten heard was, "Are you listening to me?" When Kirsten snapped out of her nap, she apologized and informed Jada that she had been up all night. Jada immediately jumped to conclusions.

"Why, what guy is it now? Don't tell me the married guy is still bothering you?" asked Jada.

Kirsten chuckled with embarrassment, remembering the last conversation she'd had about him was months ago when she'd stayed out with him.

"No, I don't hang out with him like that anymore."

Kirsten shared her activities the night before and all the details of her trip to the boat. She tried not to leave anything out, but since her brain was so fried from being up all those hours and only taking a nap, the story seemed a little short. "Why in the heck did you do that?" asked Jada. Kirsten responded, telling her that she just felt like it. She explained that she didn't feel like going home and that for some strange reason, the idea popped in her head earlier that day, so she thought, why not? Jada took her usual understanding approach and said, "No wonder you're tired. You are crazy!"

Jada knew that Kirsten planned on going home the next afternoon, so she could make it before dark. She refused to go to the club. They stayed in, more so because she didn't want to go out anyway, because normally, Kirsten being tired wouldn't have stopped her. Besides, they would stay up all night anyway. Before they fell asleep, they would probably talk about everything that happened in both their lives that they had already talked about over the phone.

Kirsten woke up the next morning a little after 11:00 and realized that her phone hadn't rung all night. Then, she realized that she hadn't taken it out of her car. She slipped on her gym shoes and ran outside in her pajamas She had missed 23 calls and 6 text messages. The bulk of the calls were shared between her mom, her sister and her old college roommates; then, she had some single entries from her dad, brother, and a few cousins. Kirsten decided to wait to return any of the calls but quickly went through the list of 'PLEASE CALL' and "are you okay" messages. She went back up to the apartment to see what they were going to eat for lunch so that she could get started on her trip back home.

"Girl, you are not going to believe this. I have missed a million calls, and I have all these text messages asking if I am okay," said Kirsten.

"Why? What's wrong with you?" she asked.

"Nothing, nothing at all," Kirsten replied.

"Well, I don't understand. Why are they calling you? What are they asking that for?" said Jada.

"It's going to be a long story," said Kirsten.

“I’m listening,” said Jada.

“Well, to make it short, and I haven’t even checked my messages yet, I believe that even though I talked to my sister yesterday, my mom somehow got worked up about me not answering my phone last night, because I left it in the car. So, she had my sister call everyone I’ve ever met to find me. Anyway, I will handle that on the drive home,” Kirsten said.

“Okay, there is obviously more to that story than you are telling me, so why don’t we figure out what we are going to eat. Then, you can tell me the rest,” said Jada.

“I’ll think about it. I really don’t feel like talking about it; at least let me call and get the facts first.

The two ordered brunch to have delivered to them, while Kirsten got dressed and ready for her trip home; she also checked a few of the voicemails that were left for her before the food arrived. They started out with her mom, saying “Hey, I haven’t talked to you in awhile; give me a call” and ended with “Please, just let somebody know you are okay.” Kirsten was becoming livid. She had talked to her mom on Thursday morning and to her sister Friday morning, and because she hadn’t answered a phone Friday night, they had alerted all of her friends and relatives, asking “Have you heard from Kirsten?” It hadn’t even been 24 hours, and she had gone much longer than that without talking to them before.

She sat and ate with Jada and talked about how she’d be spending the entire 5 hour drive fixing the mess she was in. Before Kirsten finished her meal, she said, “I’ve got to hurry up so that I can pay some attention to this.” Kirsten usually liked to keep a low profile when things weren't going her way, but this time, it was impossible. Everyone she knew was now on her return call list, and she wasn't going to get them off by just calling to say 'hi'.

Kirsten gathered her things so that she could head home. While hugging her friend, Kirsten shed the first tear of many to come. The both of them hated good-byes and even knowing that they would speak often, didn't change the fact that they could no longer hang out like they use to. Their lives had taken different paths, and Kirsten now had to get back to her own. She threw her bag in her car and headed toward the highway.

Her sister's number was the first she called so that she could figure out what had made her mom so upset.

"Aubrey, why is there a missing person file being created for me?" asked Kirsten.

"Why are you missing? You had everybody looking for you, because you didn't answer your phone. I'll assume you are okay, judging from the attitude you have," said her older sister.

"I don't have an attitude, but I do have a million missed calls and voicemails from people I haven't even talked to in months, people now thinking that I've run off and joined the damn circus. Didn't I talk to you less than a day ago? Why didn't you tell mom I was okay?" asked Kirsten.

"First of all, Kirsten Michelle Lawry, you need to calm down! You are the one who decided to run all across the Midwest without notice," Aubrey said.

"No, first of all; I'm grown and don't need to provide notice to go anywhere. I'm sorry if I made you worry, but it's not like I didn't answer the phone on purpose. Frankly, I am just not in the mood to talk to all these people, but now, I have to. Otherwise, they'll keep calling," said Kirsten.

"Don't be mad, because people care about you. You should be happy that someone cared enough to call your grown ass and see how you were doing. She only asked, because she was worried. Her daughter, who has a cell phone attached to her at all times, isn't answering, and she has no way of knowing whether or not you are okay. Calling your friends was the least I could do to keep her from driving to your apartment in the middle of the night," said Aubrey.

"I'm not saying I don't appreciate the concern, but did it not occur to anyone that maybe I broke my phone or lost it, or hmmm, here's one, left it in the car. I just need to know that if I don't talk to someone in 24 hours, I'm not going to have to call my playground buddies to tell them why, because that's pretty much what I have to do now," said Kirsten.

"Well, as long as you keep acting irrationally, you will."

"This is mom again; I'll talk to you later. Love you," said Kirsten.

"You too, bye," said Aubrey. "Grown ass," she mumbled, hanging up.

"Hello, Mother," she said in a low patient voice.

"Baby Girl… I was looking for you," her mom said with surprise.

"I know; half of the continent was looking for me. I'm sorry; I left my phone in the car last night, and I had so much fun that I didn't realize it was gone 'til a little while ago," Kirsten said. She started crying halfway through her apology. She hated the fact that her mom had been so worried about her just as much as she hated being wrong.

After a lecture on why she should call more often, she ended her conversation with her mom to do damage control with the others. Just as she suspected, she had several other lectures and even a few more heart felt conversations with people that her sister had told about her trip to the boat. She even had some vacation offers come of it. Kirsten knew that the next time she thought about being spontaneous, she would have to send a mass message to tell everyone when she'd return on the grid, which to Kirsten, defeated the purpose of getting away.

Kirsten snapped out of her memories of her trip and realized that her getaway didn't make her feel better, and she definitely could use a break now. Kirsten began to feel bad about the way she had treated the Dr. Feylds. She realized that the majority of what she had been allowed to get off her chest actually did make her feel a little better. Also, her mom would have had a fit to know that she had spoken to someone like that and stormed out on them. She imagined her mom saying, “Kirsten, that’s what toddlers do, and you are not a toddler.”

Kirsten decided to get up and call Dr. Feylds in the morning to apologize. She knew her issues weren’t anyone else’s fault but her own and definitely, not the people who were trying to help her. She got to her office just in time to start her computer up and get some much-needed coffee. She printed off her reports for that day and started dialing the number from the card.

Fourteen

"Hi. May I have Dr. Feylds, please?" said Kirsten.

"Sure, one moment," a lady responded.

After several seconds, Dr. Feylds picked up the call, saying "This is Dr. Feylds."

Kirsten immediately began to speak, and her nervousness came right from the pit of her stomach. She had been in the habit of not doing things that she would have to apologize for, so for this apology, she just spit it out as soon as she could to get it over with.

"Hi, it's Kirsten Lawry from Thursday; I was calling to apologize for the way our session went. I shouldn't…." Dr. Feylds cut Kirsten's apology short, saying "Kirsten, don't worry about that; considering my career, I run into a lot of people who handle anger much more aggressively. The important thing is learning how to talk about the things that bother you."

"Yeah, I know," said Kirsten.

"Well, if it is okay with you, I have an opening at 9 tomorrow; I know it's Saturday, but I'd like to see you," said Dr.Feylds.

Kirsten took a deep breath and agreed to make the appointment. Besides, she definitely had a few things to get off her mind, and if she didn't have to miss any work to do it, that would be even better.

Kirsten continued her tasks for Friday, being sure not to do them quickly. She'd learned long ago to use all of the time allowed to her, not only so that she didn't get meaningless busy work, but because no one liked a shiner. Kirsten worked and contemplated her evening but continued to come up with nothing. The confusion that filled her head was more of a distraction than all the bursts of ideas she would have usually had.

Since switching positions, she had absolutely too much time on her hands. She no longer spent her time researching and planning market strategies, and she had no idea what her knew career would be like. She felt as if she should prepare or research or contemplate something, but she had no idea what. Her inactivity came as a shock to her, mentally and physically. She drank coffee out of formality, because her brain wasn't active enough to keep her awake. The only thing that was invigorating to her was the fresh air that hit her face on the way to the car, which lasted long enough to get her home to her bed.

Kirsten's evening naps were broken up by spurts of watching home improvement shows. Midway into the first show, she realized the feature homeowner had a home office, which was something she had been working towards. She thought back to how her career could have gone wrong and everything that she could have done differently, and the harder she thought, the more she came up with nothing. This time, her emptiness brought tears of frustration.

She couldn't clear her head long enough to feel at ease, and as much as she wished she had someone to talk to about something, anything different, she couldn't. The phone never rang, but the tears kept falling. Every tear that ran from her face added pain to an already insurmountable headache.

Kirsten cried, until she couldn't see from her eyes and eventually, fell asleep. Her mind took her back to a dream she'd had months ago when she saw herself on a staircase being stabbed by a group of men. She could see the other image of herself inside of the room the stairs had led to. The other version of her was smiling and laughing and holding the arm of a handsome, smiling gentleman. They were surrounded by what looked liked friends and family members. Kirsten's mind wondered why she kept seeing two of her and why one was suffering so.

Her dream never got any further than it had when she started it. One image of her obviously loved life, and the other was paying the ultimate price for trying to live it. The entire night they stayed in the same spot, stagnant, leaving Kirsten awaiting her answer, but she never got it. She woke the next morning with a throbbing head and a faint force of life that allowed her just enough energy to move to her appointment like a zombie.

"Hi! I'm here for Dr.Feylds," said Kirsten.

"Come on in, Kirsten," Dr. Feylds said. She walked, from what must have been a break room, into her calming, yet sophisticated office.

"Hi, Dr. Feylds," said Kirsten.

"Kirsten, please call me Samantha. I think it will make this a more comfortable environment," said Samantha.

Kirsten listened to her and gave a slight smile and even slighter shrug; she didn't feel like talking, let alone about something as menial as a name. Her headache still lingered as a dull nagging pain, and her mind was just as blank as it had been the night before. Mrs. 'Samantha' would have her work cut out for her.

"Kirsten, you look a little melancholy today. Is their something, in particular, you want to talk about…or did something happen since we last talked yesterday?" asked Samantha.

"I had a rough night last night; my mind just went blank the whole night, and it pissed me off. It confused me," said Kirsten.

"What do you mean blank?" asked Samantha.

"Blank! There was nothing there. Then, I fell into this recurring dream where I see two different scenes of me at the same time. One is being abused and beaten and then, eventually, gets stabbed by these three men. The other vision of myself is standing up a flight of stairs, laughing and flirting with some guy and completely oblivious to the other me," explained Kirsten.

"Well, have you ever been abused in that way?" asked Samantha.

"No, not even close," replied Kirsten.

"Well, how do you feel about this dream?" asked Samantha.

"I don't know, confused, hopeless… nah, mostly confused," said Kirsten.

"You mentioned a guy. Did you just end a bad relationship?" asked Samantha.

"I wouldn't call it a relationship; a little while ago, I hooked up with an old flame, and to my surprise, he actually had a fiancé waiting at home for him," said Kirsten.

"Hooked up? Do you mean you were intimate?" asked Samantha.

"Yeah," said Kirsten.

"Are you upset about it?" asked Samantha.

"No," Kirsten paused, as she realized Samantha was waiting for her to explain. She took a deep breath and started to speak. "I mean, it is what it is. I had fun for the weekend, and no, I would not have expected such a thing from him. But, I keep running into these men who have their world and want the moon and the stars, too." explained Kirsten.

"When you say, 'keep', this has happened to you before, then?" questioned Samantha.

Kirsten took another deep breath and was actually forced to speak in detail about the married jerk that somehow keeps creeping up. She cleared her throat and started.

"Since he keeps coming up everywhere else, I guess now is as good a time as any to get the story out, right?"

"What do you mean, he keeps coming up? Do people ask you about him, or do you unknowingly speak about him?" she asked.

"No, I try my best to leave him in the dust, but other people keep inquiring about him. To the extreme, the friend that I spoke of the last time, the one I had the big argument with…well, the argument was about him," said Kirsten.

"Tell me about it," said Samantha.

"Well, I called after leaving my office at 6 and before starting my 7 to 7 shift at a plant. I think I was like, delirious, because he kept calling me, getting mad that I wouldn't call him back, but I couldn't because I was busy. I told her that he was on the other end and that I refused to click over, and she asked why. Well, I told her, and she just started yelling at me. She's like, 'You are so much better than that; you don't respect yourself, and 'I'm so angry with you', and when I told her how the relationship started and that it was over, she was just like 'I don't care; I'm so mad at you. You are so wrong' and that is when I snapped. I told her she was judgmental and unfair and that she hadn't even listened to the whole story. As a friend, I would have expected her support, not her alienation. So, I told her that if that was her attitude, she could kick rocks," explained Kirsten.

"Try telling me what happened with him; maybe then, I can understand how he had such an affect on you and your relationship with your friend," said Samantha.

"I don't know. I guess she had a point, but she chose the wrong way to get it across, especially to someone that had just worked 36 hours straight. I kind of let it slip that I had been a little bit too close to a married man. I mean, it's not like she didn't know I was talking to him, because I told her when I first started talking to him. It's not my fault that we started as friends and ended like we did. It started just because I said hi. I say hi to everybody, so I don't know what made this any different. I really just wanted a new client, and he looked like he would have been a good one. I saw him at the wine bar; my friend and I were hanging out, drinking martinis, noticing that everyone else in the room seemed to know each other.

My friend said, "You know, we should just start talking to these people like we know'em, because I bet half the people in here don't really know each other. They probably just saw their faces once before, if that."

"So, after she said that, I decided, why not? So, I looked at the guy next to me and said, 'How are you?' explained Kirsten. "Well, Pandora's Box, wide open. We talked about how he didn't know anyone there either. He bought a couple of drinks, and I gave him my card. I didn't do anything differently; I give everybody my card. He just so happened to be one of few people who used it. He was a well-dressed, well-spoken and interesting guy, and he was kind of cute. At no point did he mention a wife or any kids, and at the time, I didn't know any better to ask. Our conversations were great."

"Do you still feel guilt about the situation?" asked Samantha.

"Though I can't feel guilty about saying hello and hoping for a new resource, I don't have a choice not to feel guilty about attending more than one lunch date after knowing there was an attraction between the two of us. He obviously didn't want to be my client. After all, he did, eventually, tell me he was married, but only after dating me for more than a month and basically, figuring out my entire lifestyle. I mean, he so innocently asked me to teach him to play tennis. He just didn't need much of a lesson. He complemented me on everything, from my cute, sporty ponytail, to my taste in the perfect workout cloths, even suggesting some interesting outings the two of us should take, such as wine tasting, art galleries and introducing me to foreign cuisine that he had experienced overseas."

Kirsten paused and then, continued through the hardest part. "Then, he smiles at me and starts talking about his son… So I say 'a son…I can't believe he has a son!' I said to him, 'Oh, I should have known you would have at least one issue. A lot of men I meet now days are single fathers, so I guess the thing to do is to avoid getting married for as long as possible or get divorced. It's unfortunate; I know I would spoil the right man rotten and make him hate ever being single.' So, he says, 'Hahaha, for real,' he chuckles, and I'm thinking, did this man laugh at me? Then, he says, 'Well, you know, I figure I should tell you this before somebody gets hurt; I am married.'"

Samantha had not yet interrupted.

Kirsten went on to say, "I was shocked. Then, I told him, 'What! Stop playing! Why don't you wear a ring?' As a wife, it would really hurt my feelings to have a husband hate to tell anyone he has a wife; I don't care how cute that chick is. Then, he says, 'well, you know, we are not really on the best of terms. This isn't how I want my marriage to work, but anyway, now that you know, I guess I should get outta here…but I'll call you. I definitely think you are going places, and I like to surround myself with positive people.' So I say, 'yeah, well, maybe since you are off limits, you can recommend some of those positive men you know.' Yeah right, like he would have really given someone else the chance to have what he secretly wanted. I mean, if he wasn't strong enough to stay away from me, how could he expect me to be strong enough to ignore the expensive bottles of wine just to chill, not to mention feeding me fresh cut fruit covered in chocolate after a bad day at the office, the back rubs were impeccable and his taste in entertainment quite similar to mine. We had even gone to dinner and movies and out for cocktails. He taught me to play golf and came to events that I couldn't even get my closest friends to participate in," said Kirsten.

Kirsten took a break from talking long enough to let Samantha put together what she just heard. Samantha shook her head and asked, "Well, it sounds like it did start out as a friendship. What went on from there?"

"Truthfully, I don't know when the friendly hugs became erotic gestures or when it became okay for him to try to kiss me or hold my hand in public. Even though it made me feel sick, it felt nice. Somebody gave a damn enough to ask me how was work and actually wanted an answer. He cared whether I cared about the things he did for me or the things he said. Then, the conversation finally came around about how I felt about our relationship. He said, 'I would really like to know how you really feel about our situation,' and I told him, 'I mean, you are married, there probably shouldn't be a situation; I can't say I don't enjoy your company, because I do. I wish I didn't, but I do.' I told him about the people I knew with other women who couldn't seem to stay away from what was legally and religiously meant to be untainted. Then, he said, 'I just feel that I always initiate our activities, so I don't want to be a bother to you…' so I told him, 'I wouldn't call it a bother; I just don't feel comfortable. I know what I am enjoying is hurting the hell out of someone else if they knew.'"

Kirsten explained, "He tried to get all jealous by asking, 'Who you talking about, you dating somebody?' So, I got mad and said, 'How quickly you forget you have a wife. I know it's probably none of my business but are you trying to work things out? It might be a little late but I don't want to be Heather Homewrecker! Every time I bring it up you try to act like it hurts you to talk about it.'"

"Heather Homewrecker is a new one for me. It sounds like it became too much for you," said Samantha.

"Not really, but of all the internal feelings I had, I can't forget the friends that made me feel guilty and almost forced me to rationalize our involvement. I actually started to think it wouldn't have lasted as long without their input. I have to face it, but I hate to be wrong, so I did what it took to make myself feel better about the situation. Even after talking to my friend, Evelyn, I don't know how she knew, but she knew more than I thought I wasn't telling her," said Kirsten.

"So who is Evelyn?" asked Samantha.

"Evelyn is the only other friend I have that plays tennis. I had talked to her about the great guy I met; I told her about our tennis game and him telling me he had a spouse, and I told her we would just be friends, even though that was too bad. Well, for some reason, weeks later, she ended up asking me how things turned out, and I had to tell her we were still talking. And, once again, someone was asking me a question I wasn't prepared to handle. This is why I don't know how many times my mother had to tell me not to do things I had to be ashamed of. The blank look on my face said everything when she asked if I were going to sleep with him. The whole while the words came out of her mouth, I was thinking how in the world she knew to ask me that the same morning he had left my home. At that point, I am thinking I should have tried a little bit harder before letting him drag me to hell with him. I tried to avoid him, and I passed the test with the big candles. I ignored him when he brought the CD with all the love/sex songs."

"How did she know to ask you that? Do you know?' asked Samantha.

"I know how she knew. The night before when we were drinking I revealed that I was so attracted to some guy, and after being asked who, thirteen million times, I said his name. The name was so common she thought I was talking to another Camron that was there that night. I guess it didn't take too long for her to piece it together. Anyway, back to her question; she says, 'Oh' my god Kirs… you didn't! I mean, do you think you could see yourself doing this for awhile? Like, how is he spending time with you when a wife is requires 110% of a man's time?'"

"I remember saying, 'I guess his doesn't; I wish she did. Then, I wouldn't be caught in this trap. I just feel like someone is going to get hurt, and I want out. But, I don't want to be unhappy again.' As much as this conversation felt like an after school special, it was so real; somebody else knew of my complete indiscretion. I wasn't being judged or fussed at, but it really helped me to see that this had to come to an end. That was especially difficult after she said how nice his wife was, telling me where she worked. She knew they where having issues; however, he told me they were thinking about separating, when really, his wife told her they were working it out. She even said they were trying to have a baby. I felt so bad then, I damn near wanted to cry; I was officially Heather Homewrecker. It had to end, and it did, at least for me, for about a week. Unfortunately, his voicemails were starting to get to me again. Of all the guys that were leaving me messages, his were the only ones making any sense to me," said Kirsten.

"Were you in love with him?" asked Samantha.

"No, I am sure I wasn't in love with him; I am sure I was just infatuated that he knew how to get what he wanted and tried to make me happy in the process. Or so I thought. Even though I believed he was trying to make me happy, I realized something my friend, Robin told me a few months ago, and she didn't even know a fraction of the story. She knew I met and had conversations with the married guy, and she was like, 'Kirs!!!, you should not even be talking to him, He is a bad person; any time you would intentionally hurt somebody like your wife, that's horrible. It doesn't matter how nice he is to you, because anybody who would do that is not worth you spending time with.' I knew she was right, but at the time, I just felt like she didn't understand," explained Kirsten.

"Well, what did you say then?" asked Samantha.

"I told her to stop yelling at me; I didn't know he was married when I met him, and I got to know him enough to like him. I wish I could have taken myself out of the situation, but it's hard. I wasn't saying it's right; it's just hard. Then, she said 'He only wants one thing from you.' I told her she was being pretentious and that we were just friends," said Kirsten.

"Were you really just friends?" asked Samantha.

"Bullshit! He wanted a friend alright. A mistress; a woman who has power authority or ownership, something personified as female that rules or dominates… a woman other than his wife with whom a man has sexual relationships. I know I have been naive before, but this takes the cake. I knew that last time he asked to come over that I could resist, and I did. Looking back, the first time we hooked up, it was because he took me to the pier for drinks. I thought he was so nice, and most of the time, he was. I never really saw him as s womanizer until that last time, when I said, "I can't do this."

Kirsten put her hands to her face to wipe a few tears from her eyes and cleared her throat. She remembered vividly how the night went, but she never told anyone about it. She never wanted to admit that she had done such a thing. The truth of that night just sounded altogether bad, and whenever she thought about it, all she could feel was weak.

Samantha handed her a tissue and said, "It's okay; no one can judge you for what happened, but you need to get it out."

"He said 'Can't do what?' And, I said, 'Have sex with a married man. I just can't,' and he's like, 'Oh, you mean after today?' For some damn reason, I can't remember what I said after that, because all I kept saying to myself was that this will never happen again. My mother always told not to put myself in bad situations, and being alone with him would never happen again. I was torn in two. My head hurt, and I just prayed. I prayed for forgiveness. I mean, it wasn't like I hadn't had premarital sex; it wasn't like I hadn't slept with him before. It was like, damn, I really said no and let him do it anyway. How the hell does that happen?

"I was so angry, not only at what I had done, but apparently, I wasn't strong enough to stand up for myself or stand up for his wife, whether I knew her or not. The fact remains, I helped him make her a victim, and this bastard is doing the same thing to me. Why would he want to string me along if he gave a shit about me? Reality is, he didn't respect me, and he couldn't have."

Kirsten continued, "I talked to him less and less and less and found other things to do to occupy my time; it was working. Slowly but surely, it was working, It probably would've worked better if I told him I didn't want to be his mistress anymore, but as wrong as he, we were, I hate burning bridges. Besides, my plan was working; his last voicemail asked me out for an evening of drinks and him as a tip. Thankfully, I would be out of town."

"Well, you shouldn't ask your 'mistress' out when your wife is listening, at least not if you want to stay married… his wife lit a match to that bridge much better than I could. The relief I felt was like a miracle. On Sunday, when he called to ask if I received any phone calls that weekend, I reminded him that I had been dealing with a lot of other things, and I hadn't paid attention but didn't remember seeing his number. He said, 'Well her phone shows up private,' and I was like, 'Private, her phone, what am I missing?' Then, he tells me, 'Well, she saw that last message I sent you; we had some words about it, but I told her we needed to talk later.'"

As Samantha just listened, Kirsten explained, "I told him good luck and that I hope they were able to work everything out. He said 'Yeah, well, we'll see, but uh, I'll call you later.' I didn't really pay much attention to him, because I had no intention of talking to him again, not about that. So, I enjoyed the rest of my weekend, because I finally knew that I had a way out. The whole way home, I surprised myself; I didn't think about my guilt. I had forgiven myself, and I was so glad that I had a way out. Then, I started thinking, do I have a way out? What if she left him? Shit! Then, I was really in for it."

"After that brief moment of bliss, I checked my phone and realized he had called me twice and left me two messages. When I checked the messages, the first one said try to call me before 4:30; it's important. Being a little past 4:30, I hung up and dialed the number back immediately and didn't get an answer. I called the voicemail back to check the following message that I had previously been too anxious to check; it wasn't him. It was his wife with no greeting, but I don't blame her, even though I would have at least said hello, she just said:

> 'This is Lasey Bleiu, Camron's wife. I would like for you to know that we had a conversation about the relationship between the two of you today, and I am well aware as to what went on. In case you didn't know, he is married; I am his wife, and we also have a son together. Whatever happened we will deal with this from this point on. So, just to give you the head's up, we did discuss this, and just as I have told Camron, I don't appreciate it.'

That was it. No return number, no I want to talk to you, nothing. I thought about contacting her, but how? Why? I should just leave her be, the both of them. She said what she had to say. I wondered if she had to like, practice that; how do you remain that calm? How does something like this not piss you off? Don't get me wrong, I completely respect the way she handled it, and I feel so terrible that she had to experience it anyway. I really am sorry! But it was weird; it was almost like she was ignoring what happened. If that is the case, she is definitely a stronger woman than I am."

"Then, I thought maybe she didn't know the extent of it. He had to have left something out. I am not mad at him; I am a strong believer in protecting other people's feelings, but he should have thought about that prior to and not after the fact. I guess all I could do was keep praying to stay away, that he would stay away," finished Kirsten.

Just as she had gotten the last few words off her chest and had completely dried her eyes from intermittent crying, Kirsten was done. She had finally told the complete story as to how the old married friend kept creeping up in her life.

"Do you feel a little better?" asked Samantha.

"Yeah, I do. Even though that really wasn't bothering me; it just kinda came up. I do feel a little lighter now," said Kirsten.

"Good that you feel better about it, but when you came in, it was your dream that was troubling you, right?" asked Samantha.

"Yeah, that, and being annoyed about feeling empty," said Kirsten.

"Kirsten, I truly believe that your feelings of emptiness are a result of you having too much on your mind at once and not being able to focus on the things that are fulfilling to you as a person. I think that as you get things off your mind, like we did today, you will begin to make space in your life for the good things. As far as your dreams, I think they are symbolic of a transition. Sleep is when our subconscious minds take over, and on rare occasion, we express ourselves through dreams or perhaps, even sleepwalking or talking. What I would like for you to do is try and focus on the happy image of you, because it would appear that you are ending a troubling, confusing time in your life. As you become one with the happy image of yourself, the negative things that you have experienced will be behind you. Who knows? That may be Mr. Right with the gorgeous smile. So… try to focus on the positive, and try to do only the things that are fulfilling to you. If you have another night like last night, watch something funny; sometimes, it's okay to have an empty feeling, especially if you fill it with laughter. Okay?" ended Samantha.

"Okay, thanks," said Kirsten.

She left Samantha's office feeling 10lbs lighter and without her intrusive headache. Now, she had the rest of the weekend to fill with interesting, funny movies and nothing else that she could think to do.

She placed her car in park in front of her apartment and noticed a familiar car in her rear view mirror. She sat, trying to focus on the person in the car and wondered where she knew him from. As the image became clear, her breath paused in shock. It was Josh. How does he know where I live? she asked herself. She began to take deep breaths in preparation for the unknown, as her thoughts started to race…he probably isn't here for me. Did I say something mean to him? Maybe he is here for someone else; that's it, it is just a coincidence. Kirsten's breathing began to calm her down, and just as it had, the familiar car pulled away from the lot and drove off down the street.

Kirsten sat still for another few seconds and got her bearings. She then grabbed her purse and walked full speed to the door. Her walk said she was busy and important, and she had mastered being in a hurry in style. Her heart and her head said, get in as soon as possible before he comes back to see which door you go in. She closed the door immediately behind her and locked it. Then, she went for her patio and windows to make sure that the stoppers her mom insisted she have were all in place.

While her mind raced as to what he could have been doing outside her place, she couldn't help but think that she had just felt so much better about life and now, she felt scared. She didn't even know if he was there for her, but his nervous tendencies gave her the impression that he was already unstable. She poured a glass of wine and sat on the couch; she told herself that she wasn't afraid anymore and that whatever he was there for wasn't going to help her get a grip on things. She sipped her wine and calmed her nerves, as she watched the comedy channel.

The jokes on the comedy channel weren't nearly funny enough to preoccupy her thoughts, and one comedian after the next, she felt as though she was losing brain cells just watching it. She reached for her cell phone, thinking of her friend, Stephani; it had been days since they last talked, and even that conversation was limited.

"Hello," answered Stephani.

"Hey it's me! What's up with you stranger?" said Kirsten.

"Not much; I am just trying to figure some things out," said Steph.

"Like what? Want some help?" asked Kirsten.

"Uh, not right now, but what's been going on with you?" asked Stephani.

"Been doing a lot of reflecting. I kinda have too much time on my hands in this new job, and I am still waiting on stuff to pan out with that guy, Nathan I was telling you about, you know, the independent guy. But, I saw a shrink, as if I can't find a better way to spend my time. Oh, that's right, I can't, and by the way, I think I'm being stalked. So… enough about me, how's business?" asked Kirsten.

"What?! A stalker and a shrink, you have really been keeping me out of the loop," said Stephani.

"No, just after telling you all of my business and having you snap at me, I kind of needed to pay someone to be nice to me…I'm just kidding, but yeah. I guess sometimes it helps to talk to someone you don't know. The stalker, well, that's another story; I just thought I saw a familiar face outside my apartment."

"Who?" asked Stephani.

"That guy, Josh remember? He is the one that wanted me to watch him play ball?" said Kirsten.

"Oh, yeah," Stephani said.

"Seriously, why do you sound like that?" asked Kirsten.

"Well, I am kind of beginning to understand the things that you were going through at work."

"Okay, we knew that weeks ago when you stopped getting paid and when everyone else quit. Heck, even Joe quit, and we all know he was a superstar," said Kirsten.

"I know; I just thought you were a complainer, and that if you were working as hard as you said you were, your job would have been better. I'm kidding! Really, I thought if I worked really hard it would work. You know how it is when you find something you like," said Stephani.

"The truth comes out. I can't believe you thought I was a slacker. After all the nights I called you from the office like, 'I'm still here!' And, what about the cases I told you about that I thought were going to be so big and weren't? Dude, I even called you at like, 5 a.m. to say, 'Steph, the early bird gets the worm!' I still can't believe you thought I was a slacker," said Kirsten.

"I said I was kidding; besides, I called you at 5; you just so happened to be up," said Stephani.

"I know. I'm playing with you, but seriously though, we need to do something for you before the shit hits the fan for you, too. So, do you want to stay, or do you want to find something else to do," asked Kirsten.

"Well, you know how the story goes; I want to stay, but I know I do need to leave. I just don't know where to go. I think I'm just going to stick it out; I'll pass my resume around until I get a real job offer."

"Okay, I wish I could help, but all I can do is tell you to 'see more people or sell something,'" laughed Kirsten.

"Right, that's all they can say. It's funny, we live in completely different places, and everything is almost identical. But, hey, I am going in to see a client right now, so let me call you later," said Stephani.

The two ended their conversation, one with the hopes of accomplishing something and the other hoping to find something to accomplish.

Fifteen

Kirsten had waited all weekend for Monday to come so that she could stop pretending that being empty wasn't bothering her and seal the deal that she made with Nathan. She went over to the office and completed a bunch of paperwork before time to be at her other job. She immediately began to think of ways to move her clients over and to work on things that would get her more accustomed to her new company.

Her plan was to continue to do her contract with her old company, until she could build her business with the new one, but when she made it into the office, she was called into the conference room to hear that her contract would end in two weeks, including the one that had just started.

Her news that morning would mean her spending the rest of her day thinking about what she would do after that. She had no idea how to put together a plan that fast and had no idea where to start. As she sat at her desk, Shelly called to tell Kirsten that she was ready to return the book that she borrowed. Kirsten and Shelly talked for a few minutes about the exam and the companies they were working for, without Kirsten giving too much information to a woman only known through the passing of books. After a few minutes of talking about their careers, the two decided it would be nice to get together. They got off the phone with plans to meet at Shelly's place to exchange the book; then, they would decide were to have appetizers and cocktails.

Kirsten printed her reports to work on and completed her work in her usual manner, not too fast, not too slow. All the while, she was trying to figure a way out. She had spent the last few months in a spiral and had no clue as to where it was leading. She had learned so many lessons but couldn't say exactly what she had learned from them.

After Kirsten spent hours wondering why her life had been so divided, it hit her. She never mixed friends with other friends; she never mixed family with friends. She most definitely never mixed colleagues with family or friends. Each section of her life was almost in complete solitude from the others. She thought that meant no one had to be more important than the other; no one entity would clash with the other. It took a split second for her to realize that no one cared what she did with her life. To put things in perspective, she wasn't the angel she wanted her parents to think she was. She wasn't so consumed with success that she couldn't have fun. She realized she was a person. If she wasn't loved by all, who cares? If she made mistakes, it didn't matter. Anyone who would hold living her life against her could kick a damn rock.

Just as she smiled at her latest revelation, she saw her friendly co-worker standing in front of her.

“Some guy named Josh came by looking for you during lunch, but I told him you weren’t here, since I know you don’t hold meetings in this office anymore,” said Chanelle.

“What… why…what did he want?” asked Kirsten, with a puzzled look on her face.

“I asked if he wanted to leave a message, but he didn’t say. He just looked really nervous and left. Maybe he wanted to take you to lunch?” added Chanelle.

“That’s weird,” said Kirsten

“Okay, well, I have to get back to work. Tell your boyfriends I’m not your personal secretary,” said Chanelle jokingly.

“Well, thanks anyway, you’re a doll!” added Kirsten.

She thought for a minute about why Josh could be trying to reach her and why he didn’t do what he usually did and call her at inopportune moments. She shrugged off his attempt to reach her and went back to thinking about what she needed to do for herself.

Kirsten decided that she dated, and she got her feelings hurt. She worked a job that she wasn’t doing too well in. She forgot things. And, all of that was, for the first time in her life, okay with her. It was time for her to finally live.

With all of her new found security and her feelings toward life’s many issues, she still had no clue which end was up.

She arrived at Shelly's place after work and rang the doorbell. She was very curious as to how this meeting would turn out, because the two of them had never met. They only spoke over the phone, and even those were brief conversations.

"Hi, are you Kirsten?" said Shelly.

"Yes, nice to finally meet you," Kirsten said.

"Come on in, have a seat."

Kirsten looked around her immediate environment, and for some strange reason she felt more at home than she had ever in her own place. When she focused back on the conversation she was having, Shelly was asking what she would like to drink.

"I'm trying a new wine. Would you like some?"

"Sure, I've tried that one; it's really good."

"So, it's kind of funny that this is our first time meeting. How long have you been at the company?"

"Well, I am not with the company anymore; I went, or am, going solo now."

"Okay, what made you decide to do that?"

"I can't say it was working out to my benefit, so when someone showed me an opportunity, I took it. How about you? What made you decide to do this as a career?"

"You know, I had done so many different things in life, and I am always looking for a new adventure. So, like you, I heard about the business and the opportunities, and I took it. And, my team is so great; anything I need help with, they're there," said Shelly.

"That's a really good team to have," Kirsten replied.

Shelly and Kirsten talked for over an hour. They sipped their wine and talked about interesting clients and the people they worked with, until eventually, Kirsten had told the complete truth about her career. Her explanation as to why she disliked her old company was as candid as she could have made it, and Shelly just sat and listened, until finally, she said, "You know, I have been sitting here listening to you, and I think you are a really nice woman, and you sound very passionate about what you want to do. I am sure you can get it done, but put them behind you. They can be as incompetent as you say they are by themselves, but as long as you think about them, it won't be about you. You have to stay positive."

Kirsten nodded her head in agreement and thought to herself, had she talked that badly about them? She knew how she felt on the inside about the promises that were made and weren't kept, but she had no idea that that was what was destroying her life. Up until that moment, she hadn't felt like she had the answer she had been looking for. As she sat and listened to Shelly talk, she felt as though she was in the presence of wisdom. She couldn't help but say, "I will try that, but listening to you, you sound very wise or spiritual even," said Kirsten.

"I don't know about wise, but I do read a lot of books. I try to be as spiritual as possible. I just live my life, and I enjoy meeting people and doing whatever I can while I am here."

Kirsten asked more questions until she had gotten most of Shelly's life story. She was amazed that the woman she was looking at had dated herself close to retirement age and didn't look a day over forty. She seems to have had such an interesting life.

When Shelly had finished talking, Kirsten was filled with hope and inspiration. She felt like she did before she took her last job and before she let worry and stress get the best of her. It was the first time she had actually felt inclined to read her bible for understanding and other books that would help her to grow as a person. She remembered a time in her life when everything she ever did came from instinct. The decisions she made were good and came easy to her.

She had, in that single moment, figured out how to regain her attraction towards chance. Her past was her past, and she didn't have to worry about it nor anyone who knew of it. She could continue to live her life just the way she loved it once before; she knew now how to keep anyone from getting in the way of her dreams.

Kirsten made it home from Shelly's just in time to rest her brain. As light and airy as she felt, she was also sleepy. She made up her bed and straightened a few things out around the house before she turned in. By 10:00, she was fast asleep.

Long after she had closed her eyes, she began to picture the dream she had been having over the last few months. The dream that had been terrifying and puzzling was now peaceful, and everyone seemed to be enjoying themselves. She kept trying to look down the stairs to check on the frazzled version of herself that she knew should be there, and she couldn't. There were no stairs, just the large room filled with people. She still couldn't make out any faces, other than her own, but she could actually hear her guests laughing and talking. The room became lighter and lighter until everything faded out.

As Kirsten blinked her eyes, she felt herself waking up. It was early, and though she felt that she had only been sleep for a few minutes, her body seemed to be completely rested. Her alarm clock hadn't even gone off yet. She knew she needed a plan to stay on top, but she hadn't put her finger on it. The first thing she would need to do is to get to work and maintain the positive vibe she had going for herself. She tried to think of all the things that people could do or say to piss her off and came up with nothing. Her plan was to do her job and smile, because she couldn't be less concerned with what happened there.

She made it to the office just in time to greet the friends she had made and sit at her desk to start on her work. She completed a lot of work early and started looking online for different job postings. Surprisingly, she saw the opening for the job she had left weeks ago due to her contract which said she couldn't hold two jobs.

She immediately picked up the phone and called the company, asking for her old supervisor and left a message for him.

It would be the following Monday before he would call her back and tell her she could have her job but only if she could start immediately. It was almost as if he had to think about it before hiring her, or maybe, it had taken him that long to get the message. Kirsten took him up on the opportunity and would go to the plant the first three days out of every week from 7 p.m. to 7 a.m., starting that Tuesday. By her last week of contracted employment, she couldn't even tell that the week had gone by, but by then, she had figured out her plan. She had already been given privilege to two different financial companies, Nathan's company and one of his associates, both of which would still be commission but would offer her plenty of opportunities and they could care less what she did if their name wasn't attached to it. To her, that meant she could keep her job at the plant and work out office hours. So, she did. Monday through Wednesday, she would sleep 8 a.m. to 1 p.m. and hold office hours from 2 p.m. to 6 p.m., giving her just enough time to get to work by 7. Then, Thursday through Saturday was her flex time; she would alternate holding appointments at each office and/or do whatever she wanted. Sunday was for her. On Sundays, she made plans as to what she would do after the next 3 months were over. In 3 months, her lease would be over, and hopefully, she could quit her job at the plant. She would have the flexibility to do whatever she wanted.

Her ultimate goal was to simplify her life so that she could learn to control what she had, and to do that, she realized she had to make some sacrifices. She canceled her cable and gym membership, which for her, didn't matter, because she wouldn't have time for them anyway. She started grocery shopping for herself so that she would only have to make one trip for food a week, and most of the time, it was the same thing. She stuck to her plan as best she could, but sometimes, she ended up at a fast food place or out for coffee with a client. She did everything she could to make sure her plans to buy a loft and to live the life she had planned on living was possible.

When her time was up, she realized that, over the course of three months, she worked harder than she had probably ever worked in her life and harder than she ever wanted to have to work again. She sold financial products during the day and worked half of the week at night. She saved every penny that she made from her sales and a few from her night job, making her net worth go from a negative number to allow her to live comfortably, and had more to come. With her financial situation looking up, she had the freedom to research opportunities and find investors. Now, she could focus on what she loved; her career had grown so much over the past three months that she couldn't believe it herself. She knew it was possible but only if she didn't have to worry about sustaining her lifestyle. Now, she didn't have to.

Sixteen

After three grueling months of following her plan, Kirsten could finally do whatever she wanted to do. No more punching clocks at her 7 to 7 to make sure that she had an income. She thought back to her days when she had first gotten into the business. The phrase, 'One day you'll look back and laugh' came to mind, as she thought she definitely wouldn't laugh, because it wasn't funny. The more she thought about it, she realized that she hadn't laughed much the whole time. Following her thought, she picked up the phone to call her girls to see what they were doing that weekend; they had to catch up.

"Hey, Evelyn, it's Kirsten," she said.

"I know who you are. What's up?" said Evelyn.

"Let's meet at Niquo's for appetizers tonight at seven."

"What, don't you have to like work or something?" said Evelyn.

"No, are you going to be there or not?" said Kirsten.

"Yeah, I'll come," said Evelyn.

"Good, call Robin, and tell her to come too; I'll call Elle," said Kirsten.

"Okay. See ya later," said Evelyn.

"See ya," said Kirsten.

Kirsten got off the phone with Evelyn just as Josh was calling her. She would have ignored his call like she had the last three months except the 'press any button to answer' function was on her cell phone. She hung the phone up with him and started dialing Elle again to invite her out. She was really looking forward to hanging out with her friends, so they could all catch up. She knew, vaguely, of Robin's graduation, because she went to her celebration luncheon. But, she couldn't stay to talk with her. Evelyn had just accepted a new job that she announced over email. Kirsten congratulated her, but she didn't know much about it. And, as for Elle, she was the same old glamour girl she had always been.

"Hey, Kirsten," Elle answered the phone.

"Hey, what are you doing?" said Kirsten.

"Leaving my office. What about you?" replied Elle.

"I am trying to get all of you to meet for appetizers tonight at 7," said Kirsten.

"Okay, where?" Elle said.

"Niquo's, where else?" Kirsten replied.

"Alright, is everything okay?" asked Elle.

"Yeah, why?" asked Kirsten.

"Because we really haven't been out much, and for you to want to go at all, let alone on a Thursday, is kind of weird. I guess we do need to catch up though," said Elle.

"We will; I'll see you at 7," Kirsten said.

"Okay, bye," said Elle.

That was it; Kirsten was going to hang out with her friends, and hopefully, it would be just as fun as she had remembered. Elle was right; they had fallen off so much since the last time they got together, and even though they kept in touch via email, it wasn't the same as them going out every week and having sleepovers and girl talk. Those were things that you could never get too old for. Granted, sometimes, you have to prioritize, but it was a painful thing to put her career and her job before her friends and family. She missed that work life balance.

Before Kirsten could go out with her friends, she had to first call her parents and tell them about her accomplishments and her plans. They would be extremely happy, because over the last three months, she only called them to say hi. Not only would she have to call them, she would have to plan her next visit to see them, since she no longer had to work all week. She also had to make sure that her plans for her new home were moving along smoothly.

"Hello, Mommy," Kirsten said, as her mother answered the phone.

"Hey, Baby Girl… don't you sound excited!" said her mom.

"I am," Kirsten confirmed.

"I am glad; I haven't heard you sound so good in over the last three months. What's new?" her mom asked.

"Well, is my dad home?"

"No, but Aubrey is here; she's on her way to the airport to go back to Jersey in a few."

"Aww, that means I'll have to make a separate trip to see her," said Kirsten.

"What do you mean a separate trip? Are you on your way home?" asked her mom, Kim.

"Not at the moment, but I was going to come home this weekend. Are you all busy or something?" asked Kirsten.

"No, Austin will be just getting back from his college tour, and your dad should be home by then. What's the special occasion?" said Kim.

"Well, I was going to wait for my daddy to tell you both at the same time, but since you beat it out of me," Kirsten laughed. "I can finally quit my night job and do sales full time. Not only that, I finally have all the details worked out for my loft, and my architect has a really good reputation," said Kirsten.

"Well, congratulations! I know you had been working really hard, but I wasn't quite sure why," said her mom.

"Okay, well, tell Aubrey I said hello and have a safe trip. I will talk to you all later," said Kirsten.

"Okay, bye, love you," said Kirsten's mother.

"Bye, love you too," Said Kirsten.

Kirsten was half way down her list of things to do before her outing with her friends, and now, she was adding "pack for home" to the list. She wrapped up things at her office and went home to get dressed.

"Hey," Kirsten greeted Robin and Evelyn with hugs, as they walked through the door. The three of them had made it to Niquo's almost around the same time, and they were waiting on Elle. They chatted to each other, just as any one would who hadn't seen a friend in a long time, when Evelyn said, "Okay, so where is the ring?"

"Girl, what ring?" asked Kirsten.

"I mean, you must have met "Mr. Right" or something, because you all of a sudden wanted to get together," said Evelyn.

"She does have a point, Kirsten," Robin chimed in.

"No Mr. Right, I just wanted to celebrate life with my girls. That's all; besides, you act like I'm the only one that has been MIA; you all haven't been getting together either," said Kirsten.

"Yeah, you missed the last couple but only because you were at work, I guess."

"I'll do better," said Kirsten.

"Well, just tell us what is going on," said Robin.

"Wait, Elle is pulling up now," said Kirsten.

The ladies went to their seats, waiting for Kirsten to tell them her big news so that they all could begin to catch up after their absence from each other.

"Okay, so… I will no longer be working nights at the plant," Kirsten said. Everyone began to congratulate her, as she continued, "I'm not done; in addition to doing full time sales, I will also be investing a loft development that I received a state grant for. Now, I'm done."

"That is so good; now, we can go back to hanging out," said Robin.

"Yep, I am so happy. You all just don't understand. I have missed you all so much, and there is nothing like sitting around talking to your girls and being silly. You know, just being yourself. I don't know; I love you all. You are the best friends a girl could ask for," Kirsten said, as a tear fell from her eye.

The girls sat and celebrated the news for the next couple of hours, having their usual talks, as if they hadn't spent anytime apart. Just as they were wrapping up their conversations, Kirsten's phone rang. It was Josh calling her again. She decided it was time to nip his obsessive tendencies in the bud.

"Hello," said Kirsten.

"Hi, uh Kirsten, this is Josh," he said.

"Josh, can I help you with anything?" said Kirsten.

"Well, I really just wanted to talk to you. I keep calling you, but you never talk to me," said Josh.

"Josh, I don't really have too much to say. It was nice meeting you and all, but I am not interested in creating a relationship with you or anything," said Kirsten.

"But, Kirsten, I love you," he stuttered.

"You can't love me; you don't even know me," Kirsten said, as she shrugged her shoulders and shook her head to her girls with confusion. They were all on the edge of their seats waiting to hear what was going on.

Robin said, "Girl, just hang up; you might need a restraining order," as Kirsten continued her phone conversation.

Josh continued, "But, Kirsten, I know I do. I been watching you, and I think you are so perfect for me. I know you work hard, but I will take care of you. None of those other men you talk to can take care of you like I can," said Josh.

At this point, Kirsten recognized that this situation wasn't about to go away easily, and she wasn't sure exactly how to end it. She did know she needed to get him off the phone without pissing him off. Kirsten said, "Well, I am out with my friends right now, so maybe, we can talk about this later, okay."

Immediately, Josh blew up. "What?! Are you are having a private conversation about me in front of your friends? I can't believe you, Kirsten; you just want to hurt me. You are trying to break my heart on purpose," whined Josh.

Kirsten got scared and hung up the phone on him. She told her friends, "Okay, I really just don't understand;

we went to lunch one time, and I didn't know he was crazy. Oh my God! What am I supposed to do?"

"Call the police," said Evelyn.

Everyone nodded and agreed that she should call them immediately, so if she needed to do anything else, she would know. "Now? Right here?" Kirsten asked.

"Yeah, you might as well; besides, you don't know where he is or if he is following you. Get the bill, and we can go to the car and call."

They paid their bill and walked out of the restaurant to get in Elle's truck. Kirsten used her cell phone to call the police, but as long as he hadn't attempted anything, they could do nothing about it. They sat and talked about what they would do next, and Evelyn volunteered to stay with Kirsten until she left for home. Then, she would drop her off on the way to her parents. That way, she wouldn't be alone, until she had to get on the highway, and she could notice if the same car followed her for a few hours. Kirsten thought as for the rest, she would deal with later.

Everyone made it home safely, and Kirsten and Evelyn talked about how she had met Josh. She had no idea as to why he had gotten the impression that they could be together nor did she care. She just needed him gone. She had gotten rid of all the stressful things in her life, and she didn't need him knocking any doors down looking for her.

Seventeen

Evelyn and Kirsten woke up early so that Evelyn could get to work on time. Kirsten loaded her car for the weekend and took her friend home. Her trip seemed like a long one, since it had been such awhile since she was home. She tried her best to stay within the speed limit, but her anxiousness kept weighing heavy on the gas pedal.

After a little over two hours, she pulled up to her parent's home and hopped out of the car. This time, she would take her bags in with her, as opposed to having her little brother get them when he came home. Kirsten walked in, interrupting her mom's meeting with one of her friends she was going into business with. "Hello, Mother," she said, with a big smile on her face. Her mom replied, "It's my baby girl" and immediately introduced her to her partner.

"Okay, well it was nice to meet you; I'll let you two finish," she said.

"We'll be done soon; I'll come up in a bit," replied her mom. Kirsten nodded and took her weekend bags up to the guest room that she had claimed as her own.

Her mom came up the stairs after only a few minutes, saying "You knew I wouldn't be long knowing you came all the way home to see me."

"I know; I didn't think you had a meeting though, or I would have waited," said Kirsten.

"Why are you so early? You must have driven through all the rush hour traffic trying to get here. Kirsten definitely wasn't going to tell her mom why she was really early, not in the first couple of minutes of her being there. Then, she would just worry about her the rest of the trip.

"No, most of the traffic comes into the city so I didn't run into much. Before you say anything, don't ask me what I want for dinner, because I am taking you and dad out," said Kirsten.

"Oh, really, where are we going?" said her mom.

"I don't know. Want to go to Chicago?" asked Kirsten.

"Wherever you want to take me," her mom replied.

Kirsten and her mom left home to run errands until her dad had gotten off his shift from work; she couldn't wait to tell him the news about her finally reaching her goals. She and her mom shopped and went for lunch during the day and left for dinner shortly after her dad got home.

"Okay, since I have your attention, I came up here to tell you that I quit my night job at the plant."

"That's good, right?" asked her dad.

"Yeah, I can do full time sales now," said Kirsten.

"Oh no, Kirsten, we have been here before, and I don't like where this is going. What happens when you realize that commissions don't come when you want them to come? What happens then; you'll be trying to find another in-between job," said big Austin.

"I knew you would say that, and then, that's when I'd tell you that I have made a bunch of money since all the drama from a few months ago. And, I found a loft building. Remember the one I had been telling you about? It comes with a grant for repairs to rebuild the community, and I can mortgage it until I sell the units."

"Now, that's more like good news. Go head, Baby Girl. See Kim, Daddy's baby, Momma's maybe," he said, while her mom sat chuckling.

"What's so funny, Kim? You knew about this, didn't you? See, you all don't tell me anything," said her dad.

"Oh, Austin, I didn't know until she told me, and we tell you stuff all the time; you just don't listen," said Kim.

Kirsten smiled, as she listened to her parents go back and forth; she was so happy that this time, she was able to deliver some good news. Her happiness about her good news was short lived when she thought about having a stalker. The idea had popped into her head a few times that day, and she couldn't put her finger on the answer. She was less afraid of him than her just wanting him to go away.

“Dad, you’re a cop!” Kirsten said, as if she just realized it.

“Kirsten, I’ve been a cop for longer than you could remember. Why are you all of a sudden intrigued by it?” her dad said.

“Um, okay, I have a question. What do people do to get rid of stalkers?” asked Kirsten.

“What?! Do you have a stalker?” asked her dad.

“Well, yeah, I called the police there, but they said they couldn’t do anything unless he tried something so…” said Kirsten.

“Who the hell is this guy? It is a guy, right? How long has he been stalking you? What is he doing?” asked her dad.

“Dad, you can calm down; it’s not that bad. He hasn’t done anything yet; he just said that he was like, in love with me and that he had been watching me... I just want to get rid of him,” said Kirsten.

“So, you’ve talked to him? You know who he is?” asked her dad.

“Yeah, I know his first name is Josh; I went to lunch with him months ago, more like at the beginning of last year, but I only spoke to him last night when he said that he loved me and that I was hurting him,” she explained.

“What do you mean, hurting him? Kirsten this is serious. Who was the officer that said they couldn’t do anything?” asked her dad.

"I don't remember, but I wouldn't even know how to find him if they could," replied Kirsten.

"Look, Kirsten, I worry about you kids, especially you girls, but at least your sister is with Devin. You are down there by yourself. I think it's time you think about coming home," her dad said.

"Daddy, I'm not coming home for this. If I move home every time I have a problem with some guy, my life would suck. I'm fine; I know how to take care of myself, and I keep trying to prove it to you. Every time something happens, you want me to come home. I'm sorry, but I'm too old for that," Kirsten defended.

"Kirsten, we are not saying that you can't take care of yourself; we just want you to be safe," said her mom.

"Your mom is right, you know. I am proud of you and all that you have accomplished, and you don't have to keep trying to prove stuff to me, to us. Like she said, your mom and I just want you to be safe, and if that means wanting you home, you can't be mad at me for asking," said Dad.

"Dad, I'm not coming home; maybe, I'll get a gun permit or something. Besides, I'm getting ready to move anyway, so let's just enjoy dinner. I will take care of it when I come get back," said Kirsten.

"Okay, Kirsten, have it your way. But, of course, you were going to anyway, right? I don't understand how someone so smart could have such a hard head."

"But, Daddy, I…" Kirsten started.

"But, Daddy, what?" asked her dad.

"Austin… Kirsten, we can talk about this at home," said Kirsten's mom.

Kirsten poked her lip out momentarily, until her mom's stern look reminded her of being scolded for acting like a toddler. She saw the waiter and immediately turned on the charm, saying "excuse me, would you bring us two glasses of chardonnay and another cognac please." The waiter nodded his head and went off to honor her request.

The three sat at the table and waited for their meals to come. Kirsten's parents were obviously disturbed by their previous conversation. Her mom put on her best corporate smile so that she could look to be in good spirits, and her dad started a new conversation in his usual way by asking, "So, how's your car running?"

"Great, now that it's paid off," she replied.

"So, tell me how you managed to do all of this," her dad finally asked.

"I just kept hearing really successful people say to simplify my life you should eliminate distractions and avoid commitments, so I did. I set my mind to what I wanted to do and how I could do it. So, whenever something came up, I would just think of what I was trying to do and handle whatever it was, so I could move on with my plan," Kirsten said.

"Your whole life is made of commitments; this sales thing is a commitment," Replied her dad.

"Actually, being a tycoon is a commitment; the financial sales just gets me there. I just set a tight schedule for myself and stuck to it. Once I didn't have to worry about making money, and I could offer advice to people without all the pressure, I just started to make more. I was able to focus on more opportunities," said Kirsten.

"Takes money to make money, huh?" her mom exclaimed.

"Yeah, I guess it sure does," she replied.

The Lawry family returned to their home after their dinner outing, just about ready for a good nap. The younger Austin had other things planned. He had been waiting for one of his family members to return, so they could watch his idea of a funny movie.

At nearly 10:00, Kirsten's phone began to ring back to back; each time it went between UNKNOWN and PRIVATE. She normally didn't answer those calls, but after about 20 minutes of the annoyance, she did, just to get to the bottom of it.

"Kirsten, why don't you answer when I call you? You know I miss you," said the man on the other end.

"Is this Josh?" she asked.

"You know exactly who this is; I just don't understand. What did I ever do to you?" he said.

"Look, I'm not trying to hurt you but…" Kirsten started.

Her dad grabbed the phone with a level of authority that she had never seen before. Sure, she had been punished by him before, and she had seen him fuss at her younger brother but usually with a calm and controlled demeanor. He snatched Kirsten's phone and with the same ferocity said, "Look here, Josh; this is Kirsten's dad. I have heard that she asked you to leave her alone, and if you think I'm going to let your little punk ass keep harassing my child, you got another thing coming. You are going to hang up this phone and refrain from ever contacting her again. SHUT UP! I'm talking! If she so much as sees you across the street, you better start praying that you die of natural causes before I get to you. You understand me? " yelled her dad.

"But, but, but sir," stammered Josh.

"Do you understand me?" her dad asked again.

"Yes, yes, I understand," said Josh.

Her daddy slammed the phone shut, turning it off. He immediately turned to walk out of the family room, leaving everyone with their jaws wide open and faces stunned. Kirsten knew her daddy was a hero, but she had never seen it so up close and personal. He had done a really good job at sheltering them, so he really never had to show his protective side.

Kirsten, her mom and her brother, Austin sat in silence for about 10 seconds, until Kirsten said "Whoa!" which was followed by her little brother's "Man! He snapped." Her mom just sat there, still trying to rationalize with what she had just seen.

"Who is this Josh dude?" Austin asked.

"Some guy who is stalking me; he says he loves me," said Kirsten.

"Man, people are so stupid; you not supposed to tell no girl that. Then, she'll try to rap you around her damn finger," he said.

"AUSTIN! Watch your mouth!" her mom said.

"I'm just saying; these chicks already think the world revolves around them."

"AUSTIN!" her mom shouted again.

"What? I ain't talking about her," said Austin.

"OH, I know!" Kirsten sniped.

"I don't have to take this; just let me know if you want me to get at him," Austin said, walking up the stairs.

"Kim, what are we going to do with the men in this family?" Kirsten asked her mom.

"I don't know, and I am still mom to you," her mother said.

The two women stayed and watched the rest of the movie. Kirsten curled up next to her mom on the couch, as they attempted to finish the night in what was left of their good spirits.

Kirsten knew her dad had probably done what he thought was best for her, and she hoped that it had worked. However, she knew first hand that when somebody sets their mind to something, no matter how trivial or novel the idea might be, they go for it, especially if they had practice at it. Just as she had always set her mind to do things, she did them, no matter the consequence, no matter hardship; she did it. Being told that she couldn't do it was like a knife through the heart, in which case, she was probably just like Josh. Only, she knew better than to set sights for something that another person had to validate. Whatever Josh had said to her father about understanding was fine, but unless someone or something else had taken her place in his mind, she would need to be on high alert.

She awoke Saturday afternoon, stretched out on the couch with a small throw over her. She stood to her feet and walked around the silent house, until she saw her mom in the office, reading.

"Where is everybody?" she asked.

"Your dad left really early; he said he had some work to do. Austin went to play football with his friends," her mom replied.

"I thought Dad was taking the day off?" asked Kirsten.

"So did I, but I guess he just didn't want to sit around the house."

"Well, I'm gonna go back to sleep; let me know when everyone gets here. We can go do something."

"Okay!"

"Kirsten went back to her spot on the couch and grabbed the television remote. She was going back to sleep, but the best way for her to get there was to watch some mind numbing TV. She threw the blanket back over her and flicked through the channels, as she thought about what her mom said. She grew concerned, as she thought about her dad having work to do on his day off. For most of her childhood, he worked every day of the week, but in the last couple of years, his day off meant just that, no work, no housework, yard work, nothing, especially if his kids were home. She knew, in the back of her mind, that he didn't have enough information to find Josh, but that wouldn't stop him from trying.

Kirsten and her mom hung around the house for the rest of the day. Her mom had been getting caught up on some housekeeping, and Kirsten had been named the designated helper. It only seemed right, since she had kept her out of the house most of the day before. On Sunday, the family went to church and had dinner with each other before Kirsten returned home. Her dad never said anything about Josh, and Kirsten never asked. She was so caught up in getting back to the city to move into her new loft and was really excited to be meeting her friends later to help her move a few things.

Eighteen

Unpacking the boxes her friends had helped her to bring in, Kirsten was in the process of moving into her new home. Living in her apartment and trying to fix up her loft was weighing on her, so she wanted to hurry and get moved in. That way, she could start to get comfortable in her new place. She bought a large abandoned and oddly shaped warehouse space right outside of the downtown district. Surprisingly, it was fairly cheap; she mortgaged it for three quarters of a million, which would be a nice piece of her monthly budget. There was a 1500 square foot space she had carved out for her own loft. She had the contractors do all of the structural changes, plumbing and electrical stuff… oh, and making sure the old ass building didn't fall on her. It was beautiful; the front door was made of oversized wood, and the back was a bolted steel door. The master bathroom was nearly complete with slate tile floors and walk-in shower walls; it looked as if it was on its way to becoming a spa. Everything else was a work in progress.

Kirsten had just gotten off the phone with her architect. Surprised that he was working so hard on a Saturday morning, he said he would be right over, so they could get started. Coming from the other side of town, it would be at least 45 minutes. She was lucky the architect also owned his own contracting company, which was small, but their work was good, so she was really getting a good deal. She unpacked her things and tried to put everything in a decent place, considering her contractor/architect was on the way to go over the plans. She had only spoken with him over the phone before he had passed the phone to his assistant to take care of her, but for some reason unknown to her, he now insisted on taking a more active role in her project. She wasn't sure why he had this sudden interest, but if he were like most middle-aged guys she had been doing business with, she would pass. They were all full of compliments and trying to gloss past the facts, so they could give the impression that they could handle it all for her and that she should trust them. It was kind of like her old friend, Mr. Camron Bleiu. He was probably someone's middle-aged husband trying to make her his escape from his dull, miserable midlife crisis.

Kirsten continued to move boxes out of the way until her front doorbell rang. She had forgotten about the intercom unit; it was at the back of the loft where she was moving boxes. She ran straight to the front with a sliding stop at the door. She loved doing that. She'd never had enough space in any of her apartments to slide around, but the feeling of freedom and youthfulness she got from it made her notice that she had missed out. At the door, stood a tall 20 something looking guy, with beautiful, dark skin a nice, football player frame and the best damn smile she had noticed in months… hell, maybe ever. She thought he must be, obviously, in the wrong place, because he didn't look like he was carrying a delivery for her.

“Hi, I am looking for Kirsten Lawry?” said the tall guy. Kirsten kept trying to think who this guy could be at her door. She hadn’t officially changed her address, and she definitely hadn’t given it to anyone she didn’t know.

“Just a second!” she said, thinking back to the last time she had a stranger at her door. Then, she thought, as long as it wasn’t Josh, she almost didn’t care. As she unlocked it slowly, she heard, “Kirsten? It’s me Will, William Anderson.”

Kirsten was relieved; although, she wondered how in the world her architect guy had gotten there so fast. At that point, she didn’t care; the guy she was looking at was fine. She told herself to calm down and be professional. Taking a deep breath from her run and slide, she opened the door and said, “Hi, Will, I didn’t expect you so soon, I thought your office was on the north side of town…”

“It is, but I was already in the neighborhood when I called you. Besides, I like it down here. I have been looking in this area for quite some time; I guess you beat me to it,” said Will.

Kirsten looked at him with a gaze of intrigue and said, “Oh, so you were looking at *my* property?”

I was at one point, but I realized it was a bigger risk than I wanted to take. You must be really adventurous, or you have a lot of heart.”

“Something like that,” she said, as she led him to the living area where she had a contemporary, brown leather seating arrangement. “My apologies,” she said. “I’ve yet to buy the appropriate work space, so I hope you won’t mind terribly to work from your lap.” Kirsten was perfectly fine waiting to furnish her new loft. She had rushed through so many other things, but this, this was one of her dreams, and she wanted it to be perfect.

"No, I don't mind; I'm used to it. So… let's get started," he said, while rolling the blueprints out in front of her.

Having her own loft and property development firm was something that Kirsten had been dreaming of. She had waited long enough for her career to take off to finance it, and now, she had it. Even though she was anxious to get things done, she wanted to make sure she got things right.

"Before we do, can I get you something to drink, water, soda, coffee?"

"Water would be nice," her guest said. As Kirsten headed towards her refrigerator, she felt Will's eyes follow her before he himself was reminded that he was doing business. It was obvious they had an attraction to one another. Will was intrigued; not only was she beautiful, she was smart and to him, she had a glow that was almost unimaginable, but he was working and was a stronger man than to let some woman come between him and his work.

Kirsten handed him the bottle of water and a glass of ice, as he said, "You know, Kirsten, you don't have to do all of this planning on your own."

"Oh, really? I thought that was what I had you for?" replied Kirsten.

"True," said Will, "but if you lay out the floor plan and do a preliminary appraisal on the unit plans, you can sell the units before they are even completed. Preliminary sales give people the ability to make options on the property, and they love that."

"Who do I hire for that?" asked Kirsten.

Will laughed and said, "That's one of the things I do for a living. I tell you what, if you let me buy the first unit for sale, I will make sure you learn all about it."

As pleased as Kirsten was to have a potential buyer and someone who wanted to help, that didn't mean they had a deal. Kirsten wasn't too certain about the guy she was looking at; they had just met, and she didn't know him from anybody else on the street. "I'll have to see about that," she said with her most convincing, flirty, 'I 'm not a fool' smile. He smiled back and agreed.

After looking over the blueprints for the building, Will and Kirsten took a walkthrough of the entire facility. They were looking for architectural jewels to highlight in the units. After Will asked Kirsten what made her decide to develop loft spaces, they pretty much learned each other's life story, and they were like instant friends…professional friends.

Kirsten changed from her jeans into a suit after her early morning with the architect and went on an appointment of her own. Even though she really didn't like setting Saturday appointments, she did it for her good clients. She loved that she was able to set her own schedule again and that she had gotten into the position where she didn't have to waste her time on people who were not interested in doing business with her. She walked out front to her illegally parked vehicle and headed off to see her soon to retire client.

As she drove through the suburbs to the far west side of town, she couldn't help but think how awkward it was to have to work from the couch. Though her guest said he was fine with it, she made the assumption that he was trying to be nice. She was well aware of her list of priorities, but she hated for things not to be just right. Besides, she had nothing else planned for her Saturday anyway.

Kirsten's thought was broken by the sound of symphony music playing on her cell phone which was what she had programmed for her business partners. She reserved jazz for her parents and new popular songs for her friends. Everyone else just had a beep. She liked the clean sound her tunes. They had edge; they sounded refined and tasteful. On the other end of the phone, she heard, "Hi, Kirsten, it's Will. How about we get together before next week is over? If you are interested in pre-sale, we should meet with the real estate agent, attorney and accountant. Do you think you can make that happen?" said Will.

Surprised he had called so soon, Kirsten was very excited to meet with him, but she refused to show it with her reply. "Will, aren't we being a little presumptuous? I tell you what, let me do a little research, and I will get back with you. If everything is okay, when's the best time to meet with you?"

Will wasn't shocked at all to here her say what she did. From their first meeting, he knew she was the kind of person to check all the facts. He replied, "Thursdays work best for me, preferably in the afternoon."

Kirsten smiled to herself, simply because she liked holding the ball in her court when she had to make decision, and she definitely had the ball.

"Sure, I'll give you a call. Thank you," said Kirsten.

"It was my pleasure Ms. Lawry. Good bye!" Will followed. With that the conversation was over.

Kirsten had already reached her client's home. She stepped from the car and pulled her briefcase out of the backseat. Her appointment would be less than an hour, and then, she could do a little shopping. She walked up the driveway, past her client's car and another she had never seen. Her client had guests; her youngest son and his new wife were there. Surprisingly, the slightly bitter woman, who only ever wanted to talk about her retirement fund, now wanted to work on an estate plan. Kirsten finished the retirement plan business and went on to ask a bunch of questions about her estate. Her client's son had been doing some talking with his mom. I guess it took him to tell her she couldn't save everything in a jar behind her flowers. Though Kirsten was quite pleased with the new development, she wasn't about to spend her Saturday doing a bunch of work that someone made up for her. She didn't know if they were serious, and to keep her sanity, she only closed business on the weekends, not open new cases. Otherwise, she would spend her whole weekend working on it. She knew that stress was the wrong thing to introduce into a weekend. Over the past couple of months, she had learned to bait her work, get the facts first and remember to say, "I'll research what's best." Then, she'd tell them the good and bad and what she could do to fix their problem in the next appointment, which was usually when they all of a sudden remembered a material fact. Usually by the third or fourth appointment, they were satisfied. This lady had been holding off for too long; it took 6 meetings to get her final signature, not to mention the cancellations.

Kirsten wanted to do what was best for her clients, but apparently, they didn't care to waste her time in the process. Kirsten got over it though; the pay was worth it. Now, anything else was a bonus.

She ended her appointment after finding out what her client's goals were and headed off to have some fun.

"Hey, Evelyn, it's Kirsten," she said into her cell phone. "Hey, what's up?" Evelyn replied.

"Uhm, I'm on the west side, and I am planning on driving up to the home stores at the mall. I need some stuff for the loft. Wanna go?"

Evelyn sounded excited, as she said "Shopping you can always count me in."

"Okay, I'll see you in 15."

Kirsten was excited; her taste had always been expensive but simple. Evelyn, however, had expensive, trendy taste and knew how to bargain shop, which would give a nice, warm atmosphere for the loft, without spending all of the money she had for decorations. The only conflict was that Kirsten liked to sit down and map out what she wanted; Evelyn just bought stuff on a whim.

Kirsten pulled up to Evelyn's place slightly earlier than she thought she would. She jumped out to go to the rest room, as she saw Evelyn's ex boyfriend, Tre, leaving.

She hated him; he was so stuck on himself, and besides his one stinking year in pro football, he was a loser. He may have been a sweetheart to Evelyn 70% of the time, but the other 30%, he was everything short of being physically abusive, or so Evelyn said. Kirsten wouldn't have been surprised if he actually did hit her, but if he did, she would make damn sure he was taken care of. For the majority of their relationship, people thought he was just shitty, because he wasn't getting any. Everybody knew that Evelyn was one of the few adult virgins to exist. I guess they were all wrong to think that Tre wasn't getting any, because he definitely got caught cheating, several times.

"Why is he here? Why are you not dressed?" Kirsten said, as she walked into her friend's place, heading straight for the bathroom.

"Hello to you, too, jerk. You have been yelling since you got here," said Evelyn.

"Uh, yeah, because I pull up to your house to see only the biggest jackass you have ever dated leaving with a smirk on his face. You're not dressed!" said Kirsten.

Evelyn laughed at her seemingly irate friend and said, "Shut up and listen, cause you are definitely tripping for no apparent reason. He is not even my boyfriend; we are just cool. The only reason that I'm not dressed is because my garbage disposal blew up in my face, and he came to fix it. Not as if it was any of your business why he was here, but as you can see, I just got cleaned up. That is why I am still changing clothes and why he was smirking. So, don't come in here acting like my mother!"

Kirsten wiped the egg of her face long enough to say, "Well, dang, get dressed, and let's go. Don't ever scare me like that again!"

As Evelyn started putting together her clothes, she said, "I can't believe you think I would do something like that. As long as I have been staying away from him, I definitely am not just gonna give up like that. Besides, we can still be friends. You are just unbelievable!"

"Oh Evelyn, just get dressed so we can go," Kirsten said.

The two walked to the car and headed off for their shopping trip. "You are shopping for something every time I talk to you. What are you going to get now?" asked Evelyn.

"Stop lying," Kirsten said. "I was only shopping the last time, and that wasn't for the house. It was for a dress for your last minute night on the town," reminding Evelyn of the night she had decided they didn't go out together enough. She wanted to go to an Alumni party for some fraternity. Kirsten didn't even consider going. Not being the hottest single person there, she didn't meet anybody that she liked, but she knew she looked good.

"Oh, whatever," Evelyn replied. "You are either shopping for your loft, a gift for somebody, or looking for some damn boy to hang out with. Like I said, you are always shopping. When do you ever work?"

When Kirsten talked to her friends, they never really talked about work. They just wanted to have fun or talk about something that had to do with them, not their jobs. They were completely unrelated to one another, and no one knew anything about the other's profession. Kirsten looked at her as if looks could kill and said, "I don't believe you! I work all the time, hell more than any of you, and no, I'm never working when I talk to you, because I stop working… to talk to you."

"I am just messing with you," said Evelyn. The two pulled into the mall and went straight for the home stores.

They had been to every store in the mall, and all they found were some pillows and a lamp. Well, Evelyn found a bunch of stuff that Kirsten just really didn't like; at least she felt semi warm about the lamp and the pillows. Kirsten knew better than to shop with someone else anyway. She was more worried about what Evelyn thought of her taste and what was fashionable than what she really liked. Kirsten took Evelyn home and decided to swing by her apartment to grab more of her things.

Nineteen

Kirsten pulled into the parking lot of her apartment and following the discontent of not finding a parking space, she decided to stay the night at her loft. She parked illegally out front in the 20 minute loading zone and went to grab a few things. She took down a few boxes of books to give off the illusion that she really was loading stuff and went back up to take the book shelf apart for it's journey to it's new home. Besides, that would give her something to do while she daydreamed of her knew space. She grabbed a sandwich bag to put the loose pieces in and began taking out screw after screw, when she heard a knock on her door.

Company was not a usual thing for Kirsten, especially unexpected company. She didn't feel at home in her own place, so there was no way she could make someone else feel welcome. On the way over, she wondered who could be at her door and why, and if it was some kid selling magazines, she'd tip them to leave. She had just saw on the news a few days ago, how children were kidnapped and promised a lavish lifestyle and a world of freedom in exchange for selling door to door magazines. In reality, they were treated terribly and abused if they didn't sell. That explained how they were able to look so sad and beg so hard for the sale. Then, she thought maybe if it is a child, she should ask where their parents are and offer to help them. She looked through the peephole, seeing only the corner of a small piece of paper.

Kirsten grumbled aloud to herself, "Argh! I hate it when they drop these stupid food flyers of at my door. I have a million menus for a million restaurants, and dropping it off at my door isn't going to make me want it." She huffed, as she opened the door. She thought if she could open it soon enough, she could politely say, "Please don't leave me anymore flyers," but as she saw the tall, dark figure disappear out of the doorway, she realized she was moving out soon anyway. Maybe, the next person would like it.

She pulled the flyer off her door and glanced at it. It wasn't flyer…

She slammed the door shut and ran for her phone to call the police. She was shaking, holding a piece of paper that said:

> "I HATE YOU NOW! You should have opened the door; you should have just tried to talk to me. You would see that I am really a good man and that we could really be good together. We'll be together, you'll see."

The police showed just in time to keep Kirsten from losing her mind about the situation and hopefully, in time enough to catch the idiot who was stalking her. This damn Josh dude was getting on her nerves and now, was getting too close.

Two Days Later…

The move went along as planned, but Kirsten still needed to be sure that she could sell the units. As she remembered her research agreement with her architect, she pulled out her to do list to jot it down before she could forget. With her most recent course of events, her mind was backlogged, even though she knew she shouldn't let her stalker get to her. Besides, she had floor plans and sales agreements to work on. She promised herself months ago that nothing would come between her and her money. Not to say that it was a priority, it shouldn't have to be, since success should be effortless; it had no ranking in her pursuit of happiness. She could do her work and live and love all at the same time.

Kirsten grabbed her cell phone to text Will, her architect. She sent, "Will, let's get together. I found some comparables, and I would appreciate your help looking over them. Besides, I'd like to show you the plans for the bathroom, since you are my contractor, too."

Kirsten flipped through her home décor book while waiting for Will's reply. She had marked out the fixtures that she wanted for her bathroom. He replied quickly with, "I can meet with you this afternoon around 5; is that okay?"

Kirsten replied, "Can we make it 5:30? I have a 4:00, and I will need about 30 minutes to get to the loft."

She put her phone down in just enough time to see him send 'K' to say that he would be there.

Kirsten grabbed her briefcase and headed off to her uptown office for her first few appointments. When she completed them, she could get some research done before meeting with her architect. She didn't need to be at her eastside office until her 4:00, so she had a little time to learn something about selling her lofts. Kirsten didn't mind traveling from office to office, because it was much better than her days of traveling from appointment to appointment. She was pleased that she had the opportunity to work with a few different people. She was learning something new from all of them, and they were definitely keeping her in business. All she could say was that she had good karma, because all of her hard work was paying off, despite the corporate misfortune she'd had a few months ago.

Kirsten arrived at her first stop and prepared for an office meeting. She grabbed her notepad out of her briefcase and went straight for the fridge to grab a mocha frappuccino to make sure she was alert. She hated to miss out on the things that this particular senior partner had to say, because he always had something helpful that either gave her an idea or helped her solve a problem. He was quite influential, so Kirsten made sure to be in the beginning of the meeting when he spoke. Then, she snuck out immediately after to get to her own appointments. She had only stayed a few times and regretted it every time.

Kirsten made it through her appointments and even made two sales before going off to research ways to pre-sell loft developments before having them completed. Her meeting with her architect had been on her mind the whole day, except for in her last meeting, when all she could think about was the lunch she had worked straight through. To her, business was business, and lunch could wait. She was just lucky that she was closing a deal and that she didn't have to explain anything. She ate pretzels from the vending machine, while researching her tactics and eventually, looked at her clock to see that it was 4:15; her appointment was late. She picked up the phone to make sure that everything was fine, only to find that the couple she was meeting with were stuck in another meeting with their accountant. They had scheduled all the meetings on the same day and hoped that Kirsten would wait for them. Kirsten had to reschedule for early the next morning. She hated that she had to reschedule, but she refused to miss her appointment with her architect.

She printed her findings and headed back towards her loft for her meeting. She showered quickly and put on some jeans and threw on a blazer, because she thought she should attempt to be professional. Besides, her loft had a permanent chill, until she could have all the renovations done. She would be sure to talk about that with her contractor as well.

Kirsten was stacking her magazines on her coffee table after removing them from the table in her office. She had purchased her office set and pushed it off to the side of the room to avoid any business having to be done on the couch like the last time. She even got a mini fridge to make it more official.

Will knocked on the door just as Kirsten had turned to see what time it was. She scurried to the door and opened after checking to be sure it was him.

"Hey, Will, glad you could make it," Kirsten said, showing him to the office area where she had pictures sitting on the floor, waiting to be hung. Will looked at them and said, "You should have your boyfriend hang those up for you."

Kirsten looked at him with her ‘let’s just get to business look’ and said, “How considerate of you to think I have a boyfriend. Would you like something to drink before we get started?” asked Kirsten.

Will smirked back and said, “I understand; I’ll take whatever you reserve for special guests.”

“Well, I’m all out of poison, so will water do for you sir?” asked Kirsten.

They both laughed, as she wondered where his sudden burst of arrogance came from but remembered how dumb men tend to behave when they like someone. Kirsten didn’t wait for his answer about the water; she went right for bottled water and a glass. After Kirsten set the items on the table, Will turned on his serious face. Kirsten could then tell he was truly there for business.

She pulled out the presentation of the comparables she had made for him and began to go over what she wanted. She pointed out all of the designs that appealed to her, so he could do the research he needed for his end of the deal.

By the time they were done, he was a more humble version of himself again, and Kirsten was ready to be nice to him. She may have even trusted him if she hadn’t reminded herself of how much of her livelihood was wrapped inside of the deal they were working on. She was more interested in his ideas and presentation than she had been in anything in a long while, so much that she ignored the incoming calls she had received, thinking if it’s important, they’ll leave a message.

"I see that you have upgraded your work space; it's coming along nicely," said Will.

"Yeah, I have been working on it. I am thinking about having an open house soon; all my friends have been asking about a party. I think I'll make that my first one," Kirsten replied.

"You mean house warming, right? Open house is what you need to plan to get these units sold," replied Will.

"Right, but I really just meant a nice little mixer. Since you say that, I do need to plan one of those, too. What do you think if I had them on the same day? Like, if I were to have the open house in the afternoon and then, the after party in the evening, just in my unit," she said.

"What?" he asked.

"You know, we could do an open house and have a tour of the entire building. Then, with the spaces we have carved out, we could show virtual tours of what it could potentially look like. That way, people can see themselves living in the space. Of course, after they all leave, I'll tidy up, and I can just have my friends over for the party."

"I see, but when do you plan on doing this? You make it sound like it is going to be soon," he said.

"Yeah, it is. The kitchen is almost done, and the materials for the bathrooms are all in stock. How long does it take to finish a bathroom?" she asked.

"Maybe a week?" he estimated.

"Then, it's set; I'll have the party in two weeks," she insisted.

"You are pushing it. You know that right?" he said, while grabbing his things.

"I always push it; that's how I got here. Besides, all you have to do is get your crew in here to do the bathrooms and finish the kitchen. I'll do the presentations and the cosmetic stuff," she said.

"On one condition, I have to be invited to the after party," Will said.

"Of course, all of my friends are," she smiled, as she grabbed the handle to her door to let him out.

She was now filled with the type of anxiety she loved. She had something exciting to work on with an approaching deadline and a good idea as to how she was going to tackle it. She returned to her seat in the work area, first checking the voicemail she had missed during her meeting. Pushing play, she heard, "Hey Kirsten, it's uh, it's Josh. I know I had an agreement with your dad. But, it's just been so hard to stay away like this. We really uh, we really had some good times, and I still really love you, you know? Call me back. Just call me back, Kirsten. WHY? Just tell me why you want to keep us apart?"

The message ended with a slammed phone after going from a low and nervous voice to his screaming, crazy voice. She sat in her seat, thinking how extremely tired of him she was. She had thought her dad's threats may have worked after a few weeks with no attempts, but she was obviously wrong. That was it! She had to get rid of him! She had also thought about getting an engagement ring, so at least the psychos she would meet later would think she had someone close to her for protection. She saved the message so that if anything happened to her, there would be a trace to him. She ignored her urge to immediately call her dad and settled on taking care of it herself. Besides, there was nothing he could do but worry. Pushing the phone aside, she pulled her laptop in front of her; she was set on planning and making her schedule for the next two weeks to be sure everything was done.

After a horrible night of trying to sleep, Kirsten woke up with a list of things to do and people to see. Her loft had to be fully furnished, invitations had to be sent and she had to figure a way to get rid of her stalker. She got dressed and started her day by calling her friends to help her with planning the party. After her calls, she set off to the gun shop downtown to see what it would take for her to get a gun permit. She didn't think she would have to use it, but she wasn't quite sure how else to protect herself. When she was younger, she pretended to be a secret agent, having to protect people who were innocent. However, having to protect herself was scary, and she had no idea where to start. She kept thinking, was she really prepared to shoot someone? If she had to, would she have to think about it the rest of her life? Her questions were soon answered by the thought that if Josh found her, she wouldn't have much of a life. She proceeded to the gun shop and started by looking around at the handguns. Each one that she picked up brought a dose of reality to her.

"I can't shoot anybody!" she said to herself aloud.

Kirsten left the gun shop and headed to the furniture and accessories store. She needed to get started on her loft to make sure it was ready for her parties, and the thought of having to shoot someone wasn't doing justice for her. She shopped for hours, marking off her list of each room in the loft. She left the store with a large order to be delivered and an even larger list of work to do.

Twenty

At her loft, Kirsten began to scrub off all of the contractors' dust from the renovation she had been doing. Her delivery would arrive the next day with a truckload of home décor to put in place. Now, she only had to see if any of her friends were up for the task. She called her usual three, Robin, Evelyn and Elle and successfully enlisted Elle to help her decorate.

Before Elle came over, Kirsten called Stephani to invite her to her party.

"Hey, Steph, it's me, Kirsten."

"Hey, what's up?"

"I sent you an invitation to my open house, but I am not quite sure you will get it in enough time to make plans. It's Saturday after next; can you make it?"

Kirsten had been planning on finally meeting her friend, Stephani in person. They had been able to talk at least once or twice a week since everything had changed, and they both were making bigger strides in life. Stephani finally decided what she wanted to do with her life. She was applying to graduate schools overseas.

"No, I can't get off work long enough to make that trip. I'm sorry," said Stephani.

"Okay, well, I did at least want to invite you, so I will call you back and catch up. I'm in the middle of decorating," said Kirsten, trying to hide her disappointment.

The promise that they made to visit each other once they got on their feet kept being postponed, and Kirsten knew that if she didn't go before her friend went overseas, she probably wouldn't go. She had learned long ago that you meet different people for different reasons, and no matter how hard you try, sometimes, it's just not meant for you to keep in touch. Surely, the two would try to be friends forever, but forever is promised to no one, no matter what the circumstance.

The next day, after Elle and Kirsten had completely finished the decorations, Kirsten grabbed her cell phone and called her friend, Stephani back.

"Hey! How's life?" Kirsten said.

"It's cool, you know, just hanging in there," replied Stephani.

"Sounds like you still hate your job," said Kirsten.

Stephani chuckled, saying "You know me so well, and I am actually talking to you two days in a row."

"Yeah, not like you called me or anything," Kirsten laughed.

"How is your new dude so far?" asked Stephani.

"Look, I told you he wasn't my dude; I can't help it if I happen to notice that my architect is fine. I would appreciate it if you didn't refer to him as my dude. Anyway, I'm coming to Ohio, so what are you doing Thursday through Saturday?" said Kirsten.

"What? You are finally going to come visit your old friend, huh. I was beginning to think I was only good for a phone call," said Stephani.

"Ahhh…once again, you want to be an ass. Just tell me if you are busy," grunted Kirsten.

"You know I'm kidding. I do have Friday off, but I work on Thursday. Otherwise, that's cool," replied Stephani.

"Okay, my flight gets in at 7. I'll order a rental and just meet you at your house. Cool?" asked Kirsten.

"I thought you were having a party this weekend?" asked Stephani.

"I do, next weekend, but I am finished decorating, and Will, my architect, is going to have his guys finish up the last week," said Kirsten.

"Yeah, that is so great; we can finally meet each other," said Stephani.

"Yeah, you should just hope that I am not a homicidal maniac, or for that matter, I should say that about you," said Kirsten.

Kirsten and Stephani both laughed at the idea that they had known each other a little less than a year and had become such great friends. They had sent cards and small gifts to one another, so if they were really crazy, they had the address to do whatever it was that could have been done to the other. Kirsten stopped laughing long enough to say,

"Okay, well, let me finish up some work so that I don't loose too much productivity this weekend. I will probably have to find some work to do, so I can write this little trip off on my taxes. Maybe you should be my client?" said Kirsten.

"Nut, I sell the same thing you sell," said Stephani.

"Oh, yeah! Well, I'll talk with you later, definitely before my plane leaves," said Kirsten.

They ended their conversation just in time for Kirsten to take a call from her architect. He had been trying to set up a meeting with Kirsten and her people to get the loft business taken care of. Presently, she wasn't sure what he could do other than design and oversee the construction, but she was quite content to talk with him just because. He was very pleasant and seemed to have a genuine personality. Kirsten still thought he was attractive, but she refused to cross the line with him, especially not knowing whether or not he wanted to.

"This is Kirsten," she answered.

"Hey, it's Will. I'm calling to see if we can get together this week. I found some really good info on selling pre-constructed units. So, if I could pass that off to you and see where your head is on the products I presented the other day, that would be great," said Will.

"Uh, okay. I am kind of swamped until Thursday, but I have a flight to catch at 4:00, so as long as we can get together and be done by 2:30, I guess I can make it happen," replied Kirsten.

"Okay, I'll see you at 12 noon; then, you should have all the time you need," suggested Will.

"Great, see you then," said Kirsten.

Kirsten hung up the phone all smiles; she knew Thursday was going to be the most interesting day she had had in a long while and almost didn't want to wait 2 ½ more days to get there. She couldn't remember the last time she took a trip that wasn't work related or one that she didn't have to budget for.

At the table farthest from the door, Kirsten saw Will sitting in a booth, waiving his hand. She walked over to him and said, "Hello, Mr. Anderson, how are you today?"

"Just wonderful, and you?"

"Good, especially seeing the amount of work you've gotten done. We still have more than a full week to go, and we are about finished," Kirsten pointed out.

"I know, but I want your party to be really nice. Besides, it's easy to do. You are done with the decorations. The kitchen is done, and the bathrooms will be finished by the time you get off work on Monday."

"I guess things are going as planned, huh!" said Kirsten.

"Well, I am almost done with the sketches for the other units, so we can display those in print," said Will.

"Oh, I rented big screen monitors to show virtual tours, so that will add a little bit to your presentation," Kirsten added.

“Great, see, we are all set. Let’s put this stuff away and order some food,” Will urged.

They enjoyed their lunch and got to know each other a little more. This project had turned out to be a good one for both of them, because by default, Will would get to be the contractor on any of the units that were sold, while Kirsten would have accomplished one of her goals. They worked really well together and created a good friendship in the process.

Kirsten finished her food and headed towards the airport. It had become interesting to her that she would always get voicemails when she sat and talked to Will, almost as if she had never even heard her phone ring. She checked the message and heard, "Kirsten, it’s Josh. I’m just uh, just calling to apologize. I know you are mad at me but, but, but I hate knowing that I did something to get you that way. I’ll make it up to you.”

“Ahhhh,” Kirsten yelled. “Just leave me alone, damn! I should at least be able to get a restraining order,” she added. Kirsten calmed herself down, thinking a restraining order would be the first thing she did when she returned from Ohio.

Her plane landed, and she rented a car to get to Stephani’s place, just as she had said. She followed the directions she had printed off the Internet until she arrived at a community of town homes. She hadn’t had any reservations about the trip the entire time she had planned it, and she was more excited now that she had actually pulled up to her place. Stephani had helped her survive the worst job she ever had. She sat in front of the house, thinking about how the friend she had come to visit was the first of a very select few people she had actually admitted her failure to. If Steph hadn't been there to push her along the way, she couldn't imagine how things would have turned out.

By the time Kirsten opened her door to get out, her shorter friend had run out of the door to greet her.

"Oh my god, you're taller than me! You look just like your pictures," said Stephani.

"Hi, it's so good to see you," Kirsten said, hugging her friend.

"I can't believe we finally met; this is crazy," said Stephani, grabbing one of Kirsten's bags.

"I know, right!" said Kirsten.

The two went into the house and began talking about Kirsten's trip and continued to talk about everything else under the sun, until the sun practically came up. They each awakened in the same position they said their last words earlier that morning, prepared to spend the rest of their weekend out on the town. They started out with a late breakfast at the local waffle house. Afterwards, Stephani would show Kirsten all of the good malls and point out places they could hang out that night.

At the mall, they passed a cute, little boutique with a display of dresses in the window. Red had never been on her list of favorites, but for some reason, the red dress in the window was calling her. They went into the store, so she could the dress on.

"I feel like I have a dress like this already." said Kirsten.

"Do you?" Stephani asked.

"No, it just seems so familiar," she said.

"You should buy it then," suggested her friend.

Kirsten tried the dress and looked herself up and down in the mirror. For a color she had few warm feelings about, she definitely loved the dress on her. She took it to the counter with a smile on her face. She was confident that next Saturday's events would go just as planned, and all she had to do now was enjoy her time with her friend.

By the time the day was out, Kirsten had met half of Stephani's local family, her favorite sorority sisters and had even been introduced to several eligible bachelors. She was having a ball. She had absolutely no obligations but to have fun, and Stephani had done everything she could to make sure she had.

By Sunday, Kirsten was all partied out and ready to sleep in her own bed. She would have never thought she could have so much fun with someone she just met, but sure enough, she had. She took her rental car back and boarded her flight home to her usual life.

Back at home, Kirsten got herself ready for work on Monday and went right to sleep. She had neglected her body's need for rest over the weekend in exchange for two consecutive days of fun. Now, she needed to be ready for a typical week. She had several meetings and appointments on Monday and had to sign off on her loft renovations when she returned home. As far as she could tell, everything was to her liking.

The next morning, she awakened to what looked like a completely new home. It was almost as if the decorations she had put up were completely different from the ones they had put up. Since she had rushed through the last week so much, it seemed as if she hadn't stopped to enjoy her home the way she should have. Why she hadn't was a mystery to her; it was everything she could have wanted it to be.

Twenty-One

Being her own host, Kirsten knew she would run between the door and the bar all day. She dressed for her open house in a beige suit with black accessories, which matched the black accent color she chose for decorations. An hour before the open house started, she started taste testing the display she had set out for her guests. She was ready for her first group of guests to come so that she could give them the guided tour around the place. Will showed up first in his suit, all ready to help out. He had been such an asset to Kirsten during the planning that she couldn't have done all of the work without him.

"Kirsten, have you started smoking?" he asked, as he walked through the door.

"No, that's a weird question," she replied.

"Well, there are several cigarette butts around the lofts, and I am quite sure my guys cleaned the place head to toe. They are mostly outside yours, though," Will said.

"I don't know; I'll just get them up before the guests get here," said Kirsten.

"I moved, and the guests are pulling up now, but…" said Will.

"What, already? How do I look?" asked Kirsten.

"Fine, but my concern is…" he tried to speak.

"Hi, welcome. Come on in. I'm Kirsten." She introduced herself, as her guests walked in the door. "Please, take advantage of the food around the bar; there is also champagne and iced tea for you," she said, pointing towards the display she created.

They walked around the loft for about an hour, making sure that everyone enjoyed themselves and that all of their guests had time to arrive. They were in the company of the city's best realtors, investors and contractors, who had all come to see the potential Kirsten's building held for them.

She led the group outside of her loft, along the walkway she had lined with a red carpet to each of the different spaces. They walked around the space, filling room after room, waiting for the presentations to be shown on large monitors.

The presentations were a success, and the guests were enjoying themselves. They hadn't even noticed Will and Kirsten hiding and discarding the cigarette butts. The more they saw, the more worried Will became and the more irritated Kirsten had become. She kept thinking, who in their right mind was walking around her building with cigarette butts?

Shortly after the presentations, all of the guests made it back to Kirsten's loft. Most of them wanted to pick up the press packets she had provided for them, and others were trying to figure out the quickest way to get down to business and make sure they got first dibs on the property they wanted.

Kirsten pulled Will to the side to tell him that she had moved several more butts and wasn't too pleased with having someone smoking in her building. He told her that that was the same thing he had been trying to say to her. She had assumed that it was his guys who had been so careless, but he assured her that no one on his crew smoked.

Eventually, the first set of guests was gone, leaving Kirsten to tidy and replace the refreshments for the two following groups of professionals. Once they were all gone, she had the pleasure of an hour to get changed for her party, leaving Will in her living room with whatever sports channel and an entire spread of party foods. She showered and put on her new, red dress for her party and went to the front to join Will in waiting for the rest of her guests.

"You look nice!" said Will.

"Thanks, so do you." Kirsten said.

"I hope you don't mind I used your guest bath to freshen up and change," he told her.

"No, not at all. Can I get you anything?" she asked, trying to ignore how good she thought he looked.

Soon after, Robin, Evelyn, and Elle arrived "to help set up". They had no idea that everything was all ready to go. Kirsten introduced them to Will and would have to deal with the sneaky looks and snide comments that meant they didn't understand that there was only a professional relationship between the two of them.

As Kirsten's friends and family began to trickle in, she began to have more and more of a feeling of déjà vu. The party began to look like the dream she had been having a few months ago, and Will looked just like the guy with the nice smile. She didn't feel an odd connection to him. In fact, she felt like he belonged there, but as the night went on, she began to feel eerie. Her stomach was in knots, and fear stuck in her throat like a ball of rocks. She tried having a glass of wine, but nothing seemed to be working.

Her friends approached her all at once, with Elle saying, "Kirsten, are you okay? You look like you just saw a ghost or something?"

"I'm fine," she said. "I do feel kind of weird though," she replied.

"Well, if you want to go relax, we can cover for you," said Robin.

"No, the party is going to be over soon; I'll just sleep then. I probably just need to sleep it off. Yeah, it's just anxiety; it was a lot of stress planning these parties back to back," she said, trying to laugh herself back to a social mood in order to give her friends the impression that she was okay.

Her friends left her to walk around and make sure that her guests were all enjoying themselves, and by the time she had made it all of the way around the room, she found herself saying, "Thanks for coming," and "drive safely." She even told a few people, "You should stop by and visit sometime."

After clearing the place out, she started trying to clean the mess, which had grown to be too much for her. In some ways, she regretted telling her friends that she didn't need them to stay and help her clean. However, if she hadn't, she wouldn't be able to just leave the mess and head off to bed. They would have insisted cleaning 'til all was done. She threw the trash away and checked the locks on the door so that she could go to her room and get some sleep. The rest of the cleaning would have to wait for tomorrow, because she was extremely too tired to deal with it. She tossed the dress on her bathroom counter, pulled her hair into a ponytail and threw on some pajamas to get in the bed.

Just as soon as her eyes closed, she heard a loud unnerving yell, "KIRSTEN!" She jumped, snatching her head from her pillow, trying to focus on what was going on. This was all new to her. She thought back to her dream, trying to remember if she had seen anything like this, but she hadn't. She remembered that she never finished the dream, and as far as she got was her sitting at the counter, talking to the handsome guy, which turned out to be Will. "KIRRRSSTEN!!" she heard again, as she immediately began to regret her decision not to buy that gun. She had no idea what was going on, nor what she should do about it. She was alone; all of her guest had gone home. She thought maybe one of her guests had gotten drunk and passed out somewhere in the loft. She listened to hear the voice again so that she could identify where it was coming from. She climbed out of bed, looking for a weapon for her protection and a place to hide.

After picking up a hammer from her closet floor, she slid herself behind the door to hide. "Kirsten, why do you insist on playing hard to get?" She recognized the voice as belonging to Josh. "Come on baby, just come talk to me. Me and your boy, Camron are out here, and he has something very important to tell you."

Kirsten was so afraid. She ran to her nightstand to grab her cell phone and call the police, as she saw footprints appear underneath her locked, bedroom door. As she dialed 911, she simultaneously heard a loud bang and saw her door fall to the ground. She tucked her cell phone inside of her shirt, just as Josh appeared in the doorway. Kirsten stood waiting for him to move out of the way of the door so that she could run out. Her mind raced, as she wondered what the hell Camron had to do with this. She said, "Josh, this is wrong! You know that, right? I already called the police, so you should just leave."

"I don't care, cause you called the police; they can't keep us apart. You can't stop love like ours," said Josh.

Kirsten noticed that his nervous stutter was gone; he even stood with a more assertive posture than she had remembered. "Josh, there is no us. I don't want to hurt you. I just want you to find someone that can really love you. I can't do that," she tried to convince him.

"Baby, don't worry about that. I know you stay busy, but I can end all of that. I'll be the breadwinner; I'll take care of you," he said, reaching for her arm.

Kirsten jumped away from him running toward the door, making him angry. He chased her into the hallway, grabbing her ponytail. He pulled her back so hard that she screamed, as her body slammed against the wall.

"Please, just go. Just leave me alone," she yelled.

"You bitch! Leave you alone? As long as I have been there for you! You want me to leave you alone! Get up!!" he yelled, yanking her off of the ground.

Kirsten turned with the hammer she'd grabbed and swung it at his head. He reached his arm up, blocking the blow, snatching the hammer from her and throwing it down the hall. "I knew it! You do want to hurt me! I was trying to be nice to you! I even brought that loser here to apologize to you!" he snapped.

"How do you know him? How do you know what happened?" she said.

"It doesn't matter; I brought him here to apologize," said Josh, as he threw Kirsten on her own couch.

"I didn't need an apology from him; that part of my life is over. Josh, the police will be here any minute; you need to leave," said Kirsten.

"Shut up! He is going to apologize to you. You know, you women sure do make things difficult. I didn't have this much of a hassle trying to get him to tell me what he did to you. He just started bragging about how women outnumber men, at least 7 to 1, so all the women that complain about being cheated on would be crying if they weren't getting any attention. He didn't even know me. Well, Kirsten, I'm giving you the damn attention. You and only you baby." Josh said, as he pulled tape from Camron's mouth.

"Kirsten, I'm sorry; you know it wasn't like that…." he started, until Josh smacked him along side his head.

"Josh, don't take this the wrong way…" she began, as he took out a cigarette and lit it.

"You! It was you that had been in the loft. You can't just go around following people. Live your own damn life; then, maybe, just maybe, you could get someone to share it with you. You are crazy!" she said courageously, standing up from her couch, forgetting that he was larger than her and that he had come to take her against her will.

As he puffed, walking towards her, Kirsten walked backwards, realizing she had upset him. She turned to run for her door. First, hearing his footsteps behind her and then, a loud groan, she turned back in time to see Will tackle Josh to the ground. She backed up to the wall, in an effort to get out of the way. Then, she reached for her phone that had fallen out of her shirt onto the couch. She dialed the phone and ran over to the chair Camron had been tied to. She untied him so that he could help Will in restraining Josh.

"Kirsten, I'm sorry," Camron said.

"Please, just get him," she replied, still untying the ropes.

He got up and joined the other two men on the floor. Turns out, the dispatcher had already sent someone to her home, and soon after, she heard sirens. By the time she opened the door for them, Camron and Will had Josh under control.

The police arrested Josh immediately after Kirsten identified him as the perpetrator. She stood by her front door, as Will walked over to her, saying "Something told me to come back; the cigarette thing just didn't sit well with me." Kirsten was speechless. She stood there letting Will hug her, as she watched Camron walk out of the door. He knew that she wanted to get on with her life, and after talking to the policc, he was off to get back to his.

As the squad car drove away, taking Josh on his journey to confinement, Kirsten sighed at all she had experienced that year. Getting her career together, meeting new people, and even being stalked had made a major impact on who she was. She knew there was no way she could make her life perfect, no matter what she had accomplished, but she could always love living it. Everything she would experience would let her know life was real, and now, she knew how to appreciate it.

She slept that night at piece, in the arms of her close friend; there were no dreams, no one trying to narrate her life and no worries. Perhaps, she was too tired to experience the realm of her subconscious and maybe, just maybe, she had become one with her alter ego.

Alter Ego

Breinigsville, PA USA
15 October 2009

225895BV00001B/1/P

9 780615 236926